RAINEY, GO HOME!

When I spun back to the half-blind guy, he was swinging the club again, this time like he wanted to crush my skull with it.

"You bastard! You bastard!" he was saying deep in his throat, in a kind of whine.

This time I was ready for him. I ducked the wild swing and it only grazed my already aching shoulder. He stumbled past me. I chopped into his ribs and three of them cracked under the impact. I stepped over him and kicked him alongside the head. Another cracking sound, and it was over. A shudder rippled through his thick body, and crimson began worming out through his nose, ears and mouth.

I stood there breathing shallowly, letting the thing inside me crawl down where it belonged. It was what an officer in Nam had once called the Neanderthal Instinct, the thing that helped soldiers survive against a deadly enemy. Most of us that fought for a living had it. I looked down at the pavement. Death was usually the result when you sent amateurs against a pro. I could have told them that, but they wouldn't have listened. Now they had paid the price.

Also in the SOLDIER OF FORTUNE Series:

YELLOW RAIN
GREEN HELL
MORO
KALAHARI
GOLDEN TRIANGLE
DEATH SQUAD
BLOODBATH
SOMALI SMASHOUT

SOLDIER OF FORTUNE:
BLOOD ISLAND

Peter McCurtin

LEISURE BOOKS NEW YORK CITY

A LEISURE BOOK

Published by

Dorchester Publishing Co., Inc.
6 East 39th Street
New York, NY 10016

Printed in the United States of America

BLOOD ISLAND

ONE

An uncle of mine used to tell me stories about the South Pacific. I'm not talking about your James Michener kind of stuff, or the earlier ones that Maugham did so well, or the type you can catch on midnight TV with Dorothy Lamour and Bob Hope and sarongs. The tales I heard were about naval bombardments and bloody beach landings and guys getting their asses and balls blown off. That sort of thing kind of kills the romance for those places, in the mind's eye of a kid. Charred landscapes and mangled bodies floating in on the tide tend to spoil any image you might have had of that area as a paradise. What the Marines and Army saw on most of those islands and atolls in the Big War more closely resembled hell, I'm sure, and what they did there probably changed the character of the islands for all time.

Those ideas clouded into my head as I sat there in that saloon that hot night in Pago Pago. I had just gotten back from New Guinea, where I had hired myself out to help put down an uprising on the Upper Sepik River. Sitting across the table from me was another professional mercenary named John Boy, last name got given. He had been with me in New Guinea, and I had fought briefly beside him several years before in West Africa.

"That's the goddamn trouble with these islands nowadays," he was telling me as I sat there nursing a double shot of Johnny Walker and studying the lifeline of my palm. It never seemed as long as the ones in other people's hands. "We brought goddamn civilization here. We ruined these people, Rainey. Look around you, for Christ's sake."

I did not look around. I had the saloon and the town memorized. I had been there three days, taking a rest before heading back to Los Angeles, where I had a couple of chances for more work. I was already walking around on my heels, bored with Pago Pago and Samoa, with its dirty bars and dirty whores and hundred-degree temperatures. I swigged the last of the whisky, and saw that my forearm was shiny with sweat. I could also feel dampness on my face, under my arms, on my back. The sun had set three hours ago and the temperature hadn't dropped a degree. I glanced up toward an old, slow-moving ceiling fan.

"Do those things only have one speed?" I muttered.

"Western Samoa is worse than here," John Boy went on. "I stopped there on the way to New Guinea. It's a goddamn hellhole. Weak government, poverty, crime in the streets. Some character with a German name is trying to start a rebellion there. It's all trouble for these people nowadays."

"Mannheim," I said.

"Huh?"

"The guy that's challenging the Apia government. Name is Fredrik Mannheim. Grandfather used to be a kind of king there, owned most of the main island. This guy obviously wants it back. His old man, the grandfather's son, returned to Germany and became a model Nazi under Hitler. The Jews are still looking for him in South America. It looks like little Fredrik is going to try to follow in his daddy's footsteps."

"Hell, how could it be worse than now?" John Boy wondered.

I looked over at him. He wore a green fatigue outfit like the one I had on, and I knew that under that tunic he carried a special handgun, a modified Walther P-38 that could hit a dime at a hundred yards. He was blondish and young, under thirty, and he had the most innocent blue eyes I had ever seen on a merc. But John Boy could kill. I saw him wipe out a whole squad of Cubans in Namibia and then eat a hearty breakfast with the corpses lying all around him. He was a good-looking kid, but he had part of his left ear gone, leaving a scarred lump there. He had never told anybody how he had lost that part of his ear. In fact, none of us who fought other people's wars regularly knew anything at all about John Boy, except that you could depend on him if he was fighting beside you.

"How could it be worse?" I said. "Are you too young to know about what it was like in the Third Reich?"

"The third what?" he said, squinting at me.

I shook my head. "Good God," I whispered.

"Don't pull that history crap on me, Rainey," he complained. "I'm talking about right now. It would be hard for things to get much worse for those people in Apia."

"Maybe," I sighed. "Maybe, John Boy."

"The fact of the matter is," he went on thoughtfully, leaning back on his straight chair, "there could be opportunity for you and me here."

I was not really listening. I was thinking about a girl I knew in L.A. with honey-blond hair and the longest legs in the world. I was going to call her when I got back, and take her to a little Vietnamese restaurant I knew about, and hope to spend a long night with her beautiful butt decorating my hotel waterbed.

"Opportunity?" I said, returning from my fantasy.

"Sure," he said. "I heard that this Mannheim is hiring mercs for his takeover of the Apia government. He's holed up on the western side of Upolu, the main island, and he's building a private little army there. The wages might be good."

I nodded. "I hear he's already 'pacified' a couple of villages there. By force, naturally. Just a week ago he announced that he's the rightful ruler of Western Samoa. I suppose if he wins there, he'll be here in Pago Pago next."

My heart was not in the conversation. I was seeing long bronze legs parted and waited for me on that waterbed in L.A. Somehow that seemed a whole lot more important at that moment than what happened or didn't happen in Samoa.

"That's what I was thinking," John Boy said.

"That we're seeing a possible takeover of the whole area, eventually. That's big stuff, Rainey. Mannheim must have a lot of money behind him."

He had finally caught my attention. "I don't usually ask many questions about who I work for," I said slowly. "But I have a negative feeling about this German. I'm getting to the point where I can pick and choose my little wars. There are other things going on in the world beside this so-called rebellion in paradise." I said the last word acidly. "Even if there weren't, there will be something starting up at any moment. No, there has to be more than just good pay in it for me now. I've got to have a feeling about it."

"Hell," John Boy said. "Feelings are easy to come by. Just tell yourself how great it will be to get a field weapon in your hands again, and going out on patrol. All in the land of fruit and coconuts." He grinned that All-American-Boy grin that came to him so easily, and I wondered how many of the enemy had seen that grin before having a Kalashnikov or M-16 explode on them.

"I've been sweating for five weeks in New Guinea," I said. "Now I'm sweating here. What the hell is so great about the tropics? I despise coconut milk and sweat flies."

"I don't care where I fight," John Boy proclaimed. "Send me to the goddamn Antarctic and I'll go, if the pay is right."

I grinned at his enthusiasm. The young are always enthusiastic. People don't get old entirely because of biological processes. They get old because the world squashes their enthusiasm like a roach under a boot heel. I had over a decade on John Boy, and the world had punched me around quite a bit longer.

"Uncle Sam wants you," I said.

"Uncle Sam don't have the pocket money to support me in the style I've come to expect," John Boy replied. He started to add something to that remark, when his attention was suddenly drawn to the swinging doors that led to the street. Three men had just entered, all tough-looking hombres wearing khaki clothes and combat boots. I watched them as they approached our table. One was kind of tall, and walked like he had a ramrod up the back of his shirt. The second man was thick-set and bearded, and the third was an albino. I knew the second two. The bearded one was a merc named Mueller, a South African Boer I had fought with in Namibia who was a violent racist. The albino was another mercenary, a one-of-a-kind jerk named, if you can believe it, Rabbit Burroughs. Rabbit was the kind of soldier who loved to tie prisoners up and have target practice on various parts of their anatomy. He too had been in Namibia, and he and Mueller had struck up a kind of kinship. Just before the fighting was over for us there, I had set a prisoner free to keep Rabbit from torturing him to death, and when Rabbit found out, he had to be restrained from killing me. He had vowed that if our paths ever crossed again, he would finish the job he had been prevented from doing on me in Africa.

"Well, I'll be damned," John Boy said in a low voice. "That's Rabbit Burroughs just walked in. And ain't that Mueller with him?"

I nodded. "The two bastards just love each other, it seems."

The threesome had seen us, and I watched Rabbit pause in the middle of the room, his face going long. He stared at me for a long, grim moment, and spoke in an undertone to the ramrod-erect guy. Then they came on over to our table. There were only us and two Samoans in the saloon, and a fat, greasy bartender. A TV played out sitcom dullness in a far corner, but that was the only sound in the room as the three approached us.

"Well, well," Mueller said loudly in his Afrikaaner accent. "Jim Rainey. The world is very small, isn't it? And you, I don't recall your name, but you were in Namibia, yes?"

John Boy nodded, and gave Mueller his name. "And damn glad to get out, you can bet."

"Let me introduce Fredrik Mannheim," Mueller went on in his loud voice. "Maybe you have heard his name here in Pago Pago. He is the rightful authority in Western Samoa, and the general of our newly formed liberation army."

Mannheim and I exchanged long looks. He was not much older than me, maybe in his early forties. He was athletic-looking, with dark hair, a strong chin, and a rather prominent nose for a German. He held out his hand to me. "I've very pleased to meet you, Rainey. Your reputation precedes you."

I hesitated, then took his hand, still sitting down. He gripped mine firmly, and held it for a moment while our eyes were still locked in a mutual assessment. "Thanks," I said.

Mannheim did not offer his hand to John Boy. "I presume you've met Rabbit here?"

I turned my gaze on Rabbit. He was slim, a pale-skinned, rather sickly-looking guy whose straight hair and eyebrows were snow-white and whose eyes were pink behind light-blue contact lenses. I'd say he looked sickly, but he was not. I had seen him wrestle a full-grown horse to the ground, to show the animal who was boss. He also was deadly with a gun of any kind. His bony face was angular and hard, and his eyes burned into you in a way that was unnerving. I had never seen him smile. A story had once circulated that, in his particpation in the continuing war in Lebanon, he had skinned an Arab prisoner alive.

"Yes, we know each other from Africa," I said coolly. "He has promised to kill me at the first chance he gets."

Mannheim's eyebrows shot upward in surprise, and Mueller gave a grunting laugh in his throat. "Well!" Mannheim said in his German accent. "A little rivalry between professionals, I see!"

I shook my head. "No, Rabbit just loves to kill people," I said mildly.

Rabbit's face lengthened some more, and he spoke for the first time, in a low, gravelly voice. "You took my prisoner, Rainey. You made people laugh at me. Nobody does that to me."

He had put me in a bad mood the minute he walked in the door. "I would have thought you were used to people laughing," I said.

His face colored slightly from pasty white to rosy pink. "You sonofabitch," he growled in his throat.

"Now, now, gentlemen," Mueller butted in quickly. "Let old times and grievances be forgotten. We can all drink in the same bar together without bringing up the shadows of the past, Rabbit."

Rabbit gave Mueller a chilling look, and Mannheim noticed it. Mannheim turned again to me. "Of course we can. We can even fight in the same revolutionary army, Rainey. I need good leaders. We are going to make the blood flow in Apia before we are finished there. The blood of traitors to the Samoan people, decadent politicians who no longer deserve to rule."

"Or live?" I suggested.

He shrugged. "Or live."

I glanced at John Boy, and he was watching my face.

"I don't think I'm interested, Mannheim," I finally said. "It doesn't sound like my kind of fighting."

"You've made up your mind without even hearing the wage?" Mannheim asked me.

"I guess I have," I said.

He shrugged. "Maybe you'll change your mind." He glanced at John Boy. "And what about you, my young friend? Will you take my money? To do what you know best?"

John Boy looked toward me, and then took in a deep breath. "I'll think about it," he said.

"Good," Mannheim encouraged him. "In the meantime, will either of you join us at the bar?"

"I was just getting ready to return to my room at the hotel," I told him.

"Same here," John Boy said. "But thanks for the offer."

The three walked over to the mahogany bar across the room and ordered drinks. John Boy turned to me. "Are you sure about turning Mannheim down, Rainey? He was right, you should have heard his offer first."

"There are some people I can't work with," I said. "I suspect Mannheim is one of them."

"He seemed pretty friendly to me."

I looked over to the bar, where Mannheim was talking in low tones to Mueller. I could see a profile of Mannheim's face, and I didn't like what I saw in it. There was arrogance, and aloofness, and something else. Cruelty, I decided. I had had to deal with enough cruel people in my little wars.

"I'm not talking about friendly," I said to John Boy. "What do you expect him to be when he's trying to recruit you? I'm talking about what's underneath the friendliness."

John Boy shrugged. "I don't usually look that far, Rainey. Remember Crazy Jake Murphy?"

I looked at John Boy and grinned. "How could anybody forget Crazy Jake?" I said. Jake had also been in Africa during the fighting over Namibia. I had not come across him there, but I had fought with him in Vietnam.

"Well, Crazy Jake says you should never question the motives of your employer, or examine the issues of his cause. He says we should never get political, it spoils our profession."

I grunted. "That sounds pretty deep for Crazy Jake."

"He's right," John Boy said, his handsome-kid face earnest. "You don't want to start looking too close at the people that hire you, Rainey. Most of them have some warts somewhere."

"Maybe," I said. "But I can still choose the people I fight with." I rose from the table, and John Boy joined me. "I'm heading back. You coming?"

"Why not?" he said.

We moved past the men at the bar, and Mannheim nodded toward me. "See you around, Rainey," he said sober-faced.

"We'll see," I said.

John Boy was preceding me out of the place. As I passed Rabbit, he turned and gave me a look that would have made most men's mouths go dry. "You stay in Samoa, Rainey," he said, "and you're a dead man."

It was said so that Mannheim couldn't hear it. I looked at a bulge under Rabbit's shirt and knew it was a Taurus Magnum 86 that he carried with him twenty-four hours a day, like a third hand. I also knew that Rabbit would like nothing more than to empty the Taurus into my gut at that very moment, and watch me die in agony on the floor at his feet.

"You're having delusions of grandeur, Rabbit. Why don't you give up soldiering and take up dingus-jerking full-time? That's what you do best, isn't it?"

His face pinked up again, and his hand moved toward the revolver snugged in his shirt. But he stopped halfway there. Even Rabbit wasn't quite dumb enough to gun me down in front of witnesses. I turned and followed John Boy out of the place, hoping I did not hear Rabbit's Taurus explode behind me. It didn't. A few minutes later John Boy and I were back at the sleazy *South Seas* Hotel, a couple of blocks away.

We had rooms on separate floors, and parted on the rickety elevator. I unlocked the door to my room and entered a couple of minutes later, and when I turned the light on, I got a surprise.

A man and woman were standing there, waiting for me.

"What the hell!" I objected.

The woman was young, half-Samoan and half-Caucasian, and quite beautiful. She wore a black evening gown that showed remarkable cleavage and svelte shape. Her hair was long and black, with a white flower in it on the left side. Her companion was exactly her height, and wore a military uniform with a lot of braid on it. He appeared to be pure-bred Samoan, with a broad face and almond-shaped eyes.

"Good evening, Mr. Rainey," the girl said in a soft accent. "I am Leilani Awak, the daughter of Dr. Fiame Awak, Prime Minister of Western Samoa."

I was staring at the two of them openly, my curiosity aroused. If I had been armed, one of them might have been dead. I usually shoot first and then ask questions of intruders.

I nodded, and relaxed some. "I'm impressed," I said. "If that's what you wanted, you succeeded."

"This is Colonel Siaosi Tupua," she went on in that smooth, educated voice with its island accent. "An officer in my father's recently formed Civil Guard, and a personal friend of the family."

Tupua smiled and offered his hand, and I walked over and took it. "I'm glad to meet you, Colonel Tupua," I said to him. "Now, would you mind explaining what the hell you're doing in my hotel room?"

Now Tupua took over, in an accent much thicker than Leilani's.

"That would please me, Colonel Rainey," he said

politely. "May we all sit down? This may take a while."

I hesitated, then nodded. "Hell, all right. Sit down, both of you. But I'm not a Colonel. I have no rank between wars."

"I was advised that you held that rank recently in New Guinea," Tupua told me.

"That's right," I said. "But I've fought at every rank between that and private soldier, it seems. The more knowledgeable you get about killing, the more people are willing to pay you to do it."

Leilani gave me a quizzical look. Tupua merely nodded and smiled a sour smile. "It has always been so," he agreed. "Colonel Rainey, have you heard of our little beginning insurrection in Western Samoa?"

I nodded. "My friend and I were just discussing it this evening," I answered. "It seems some German is trying to tell you how to run your country. I met him earlier at the local saloon."

Leilani frowned, and was even prettier than before. "Mannheim is here in Pago Pago?" she said.

"I suspect he's recruiting for his little army," I suggested.

Tupua, his broad face lined with fatigue and worry, sighed heavily. "I'm sure you are right. He has already hired several professional soldiers, men of your profession, Colonel Rainey, to train and lead his band of renegades."

"Does he have bodyguards with him?" Leilani wondered.

I looked over at her. "He has men who would be hard to put down if you went for him," I told her.

She made a face. "By the time we could get somebody here, he will be gone. He stays only for a couple of hours when he comes over here."

Tupua sat back further on the chair. "He is an evil man, Colonel," he said. "He spent some time in our island country as a boy, after returning from Germany with his father. He once killed a Samoan boy by drowning him in the surf, just because the boy had insulted him. But there was no proof of the murder and he was not prosecuted. His father had arrested and tortured Jews and others in Nazi Germany, and hid out here for a while after the war, with Fredrik and an ailing wife. When the wife died, Mannheim left again and took Fredrik with him to Texas and then to South America. Fredrik grew up and became a seaman adventurer. He tried to start up his own country on a small island off Argentina, but was expelled. Then his interests focused again on his grandfather's homeland. His grandfather was a corrupt but powerful politician here, and this Mannheim thinks that gives him some kind of eminent domain over our islands."

"People like Mannheim don't need reasons to take what belongs to others," I said. "I've met fifty Mannheims in my business. Some of them succeed and spend the rest of their lives wallowing in corrupt power. Sometimes because men like me help them in their struggle for domination, I'm afraid."

"I don't think you would help a man like Mannheim," Leilani said to me.

I grunted. "Don't count on it," I said. "He offered me a job tonight, and frankly I was tempted. I knew the pay would be good. And that's what I'm in this business for. The pay. I try not to get political, or take sides emotionally. It gets you into trouble."

"You didn't accept his offer, though," Leilani said.

"No. Not because of Mannheim's record, though. I wasn't aware of it, and I never ask. It's best not to know. I just didn't like the man from the moment he walked into the saloon. It's that simple."

Leilani shrugged a beautiful shrug. "It comes to the same thing," she argued quietly. She wanted to like me.

I caught her gaze. "Don't try to put me on the opposite side of some fence from Mannheim. The good guy and the bad egg. I'm a hell of a lot more like him than different from him."

Now Tupua spoke up again. "But we sense that you are different, Rainey. And that is why we have come to you."

I looked from him to Leilani, and back to him. "You want to employ me too?"

"Only for a specific purpose, Colonel Rainey." He looked down at his hands for a moment. "We want you to assassinate Fredrik Mannheim."

I squinted down at him.

"We are prepared to offer you—"

"Two hundred thousand American dollars," Leilani completed the sentence for him.

He glanced over at her, and then smiled at me. "We were to start at a somewhat lower figure, and see if you wanted to bargain," Tupua said to me.

I sighed silently, and turned to Leilani. "Your father sent you here to make this offer?"

"It was my idea," she said. "But yes, Father sent us to convince you of the urgency of ending this villain's life before he destroys our world here."

"With just a word from you, we will deposit the

money in a Honolulu bank in your name," Tupua said. "Half now, the rest upon completion of the mission."

"Two-thirds now," Leilani said.

Tupua shrugged. "Two-thirds."

I was impressed by the offer. I had never been paid that kind of money for anything. It would keep me in Johnny Walker for quite some time to come.

"I don't think you understand what I do for a living," I said slowly. "I don't do political assasinations. I fight people out in the open, people who have guns and are trying to kill me. I fight wars. There's a difference, you know."

"We are in a war, Rainey," Tupua proposed to me. "It is small now, but already Mannheim has killed our troops, taken three villages in the western part of our home island, and routed two garrisons of our new Civil Guard. I fought his cutthroats and vagrants at Savaii. We were outnumbered by them three to one. Mannheim took no prisoners. A few of us fought our way out and lived to fight another day. But his butchery there stays with me, Rainey. He and his people kill cruelly and needlessly. If he should become strong enough to defeat us at Apia, I would not like to imagine what kind of terror regime he would install in our islands."

"He alleges that our government is corrupt," Leilani said, "and unresponsive to the needs of the people. He exhorts them to rebellion in his name, promising restoration of law and order and a new prosperity. What they will get is subjugation and tyranny, if we don't stop him. We do have problems with our government, and are trying to make reforms. But what we have now is paradise beside what Mannheim would give if he gained complete control. We must stop him, and stop him now. We hoped you would help us do so."

"I read that your government is almost bankrupt," I said. "How can you afford to hire somebody for two hundred thousand dollars?"

"We can't, from the financial point of view," Leilani said. "But from another viewpoint, how can we afford not to?"

I thought for a long moment, then looked up at them. "I'm afraid not," I said.

Tupua showed opened disappointment. "But why not?"

"I'm not a secret agent or an assassin. Hell, I'm not trained in that kind of thing, and I don't want to be. It's just not my kind of thing, that cloak-and-dagger stuff. I'd sooner stand at ten paces with an enemy and we'd unload revolvers into each other and see who survived. Anyway, the bottom line is, killing Mannheim without destroying his little army would be suicidal, with the men he has around him. I could take your money and give you false hopes, but I don't operate like that. Save your money. Arouse your people against Mannheim and fight him in the field and defeat him there. That's what I would do."

Leilani let out a long breath, and showed the cleavage nicely. "We didn't think you would be so difficult, Rainey."

"Hmmph," I said. "If you really want to give your money away, there are men in the islands right now who will take it, I'm sure. But I wouldn't count on them getting the job done that you want done."

Leilani looked over at Tupua. "Colonel, I'll meet you down in the lobby later."

He frowned at her, curious. Then he rose, straightening his uniform with its row of medals. He looked every inch a soldier, and I figured he was a good commander.

"Very well, Leilani. I'll be there when you are ready to leave." He turned to me. "I hope to see you again soon, Colonel Rainey."

"You never know," I said.

Tupua left then, and Leilani and I were alone, and I had to wonder why. But in the next moment, she went and turned the overhead light off at the wall. The room was plunged into semi-darkness again, the only light coming in through the windows on the street. She stood there for a moment, looking ghostly in the dimness. Then I saw her reach and unzip her dress down the back.

I rose and went to her, and she looked up at me with those big dark eyes. My groin knotted.

"I saw the way you looked at me," she said. "You want me, don't you?"

I was taken aback by all this. "Yes, I do," I said.

"Well. I thought that if we became . . . more friendly, you might be willing to continue our discussion further."

She slid the dress down off her torso, and it fell to the floor at her feet. She was completely nude except for a pair of wispy panties that clung fragilely to her bronze hips. Her body was even more beautiful than I had imagined. She stepped out of the gown and came up close to me, and I could smell the fragrance of her, and the blossom in her dark hair.

"Let's get friendly, Rainey."

I hesitated. "I'm not making any promises to you, Leilani."

"All right. Let's not talk about any of that now." She came into my arms, and there was a lot of woman to hold when she did. We kissed hotly, because she had already worked me up. Then my clothes were off, and we were on the hotel bed together. There were some soft cries in Leilani's throat then, and a lot of urgent touching and caressing, and it all exploded quickly into a climax of arched backs and twisted sheets.

It was good. Leilani was good. We lay there together for some time, physically joined, savoring the shallows of that hot passion. Then finally I got up from her and walked across the room. I picked up a bottle of whisky, removed the cap, and swigged a swallow of it. I did not offer her any.

She was propped on one elbow now, her breasts making nice curves against her and the sheet. "All I want, Rainey," she said quietly, "is for you to come back to Apia with us. To talk with my father. No promises, no commitments. But of course we would be able to continue with this newfound . . . friendship."

I turned and grinned at her. She wasn't trying to dupe me. It was all out in the open. She was enticing me with her sex. She was offering her body up as a payment for my returning to Apia with her. Just to talk with Fiame Awak.

"You're some female, Leilani."

"Thanks. I value your judgment, Rainey."

"When are you leaving?" I wondered.

"Tonight. We have a launch waiting at dockside." She looked away briefly. "If I had a gun, I would go try to find Mannheim and kill him myself before we leave."

"You'd only get yourself killed," I said. "Anyway, he may be gone by now."

"Will you return with us?" she said.

I hesitated a moment. "You and colonel go on back tonight," I said. "I'll tie up some loose ends here and take a boat to Apia tomorrow morning. Just to talk with Dr. Awak. Not to go to work for you."

"I understand," she said.

Five minutes later, she had dressed and left.

TWO

The next morning was one of those that make newcomers fall in love with the tropics. The temperature had dropped through the night, and there was a soft breeze off the ocean that caressed the shore like a lover. The still-gentle sun filtered through palm fronds and ferns and banana trees and made golden shadows on the ground. The sea was calm and blue, with sails out on the water beyond the harbor. There had been a slight rain in early morning and even the streets of Pago Pago seemed washed clean.

It was easy to hire a boat. But before I left the hotel, I went to wake John Boy up and tell him where I was headed, in case he wondered. I invited him to join me, but he had a date with a bar girl that night and was very excited about the prospects. He said he had been in Apia recently, and warned me to be careful there. The place was swarming with pick-pockets and muggers, he said. I told him I'd probably be back in a couple of days, on my way to L.A.

It was a fairly short boat ride to the main Western Samoa island of Upolu, and I was there by mid-morning. The port of Apia was the capital and seat of government, and that is where I landed. The dock area was filthy. There were people living on boats, in abject squalor, and the fishing boats and other commercial craft were rundown and rust-streaked. Beggars lined the docks and the streets at dockside, and tough-looking men in ragged clothes eyed me as I walked through the area. I don't look much like a potential victim, but I felt threatened as I walked to a cafe to make a call.

The cafe itself was dirty too. Dirty glasses and dishes littered the tables, and there were rat droppings over in a corner near the phone I used. A skinny waiter came up to me and insisted I order something in order to use the pay phone, and I ordered a sandwich and beer.

Leilani had given me a number to call to reach her, and I was sure it was some office in the Government House located not far away. But Leilani did not answer the call. She was not there. A secretary told me that a meeting had been arranged with the Prime Minister in early afternoon, and I was expected. I hung up wondering what I was really doing there.

I walked on into the city from the waterfront, and it was an eye-opener. It was worse than Pago Pago had ever been. There were only a few cars on the streets, and they looked like they had come out of some dusty museum. Hungry-looking kids wandered the streets, and more beggars. There were saloons and bars and strip joints and tattoo parlors, and it all had a worn-out, ugly look. The few shop windows that were showing merchandise had a grubby look to them. At street corners stood gangs of young toughs, looking for trouble.

Mannheim was right about one thing: Western Samoa needed change. The trouble was, it didn't need his kind of change. That was what often happened in the world of politics; an opportunist stepped in to promise better times for people like this, and then ended by subjecting them to a worse exploitation than they had ever known before, and taking away whatever civil rights they had enjoyed in their poverty. Mannheim was that kind of opportunist.

The center of the small city had many public buildings, and the largest of them were Government House and the Parliament. I knew from my reading that the Parliament was elected, not by individual citizens, but by the votes of 9000 *matai* or heads of important and old families. It was not a British or American democracy, but it had worked fairly well until independence from New Zealand and Britain. Then everything had slowly run downhill until it had gotten into the shape it was in now.

I found a small but sleazy hotel not far from Government House called the Upolu House. There was a larger hotel near the waterfront, probably cleaner, where tourists usually stayed, but I didn't want that. I preferred roaches and fifteen-watt bulbs to aloha shirts and twenty-dollar steaks.

I was checked into The Upolu House before noon. My room was on the fifth floor of a six-floor building, and had a view of another brick building. There was a ceiling fan that didn't work, and a lumpy but apparently clean bed, and a dusty print of an island scene hanging over the bed crookedly. I looked around the room and shook my head, thinking such rooms looked much the same in Africa, South America, or anywhere you went. Here, the door to the corridor had louvers built into it for air circulation, and the furniture was made of rattan. John Boy had informed me that Robert Louis Stevenson had been buried here in Apia, and I wondered if he had inhabited a similar room in those sailing-ship days, and what had brought him to this end-of-the-world place.

The hotel had a dining room, where I had an absolutely terrible lunch. I think it was fish, but I can't be sure. I was sure I would get sick from it, but my stomach held its own that time. At 1:30, I walked over to the seat of government, a large, ominous, Victorian building with two members of the new Civil Guard standing outside with rifles beside them. It was a sign of the times.

Inside there were Polynesian clerks, Polynesian officials, and Polynesian citizens trying to get help of some kind. Most of them were being ignored. They were all well-built, rather handsome people with dark, thick hair and broad faces and a look of innocence that us foreigners had lost, if we ever had had it. The girls were good-looking in an earthy, sensual sort of way, but most of them had no money or inclination for makeup or finery of any kind.

Dr. Fiame Awak's offices were on the third floor, and I was led there by an armed guard. I guess everybody was pretty much nerved up because of Mannheim. I was shown into a reception office with paneled walls and carpeting, and it was the first evidence of wealth I had seen on the island.

"Oh, yes, Mr. Rainey. They are ready for you."

I wondered who "they" included, and was soon to find out. When I was ushered into Awak's spacious and sumptuous private office, I found Leilani and Tupua there, a man behind a long desk who was obvioiusly Awak the Prime Minister and Leilani's father, and two men I had never seen before. One of them wore a uniform like that of Tupua's, except it had more gold braid and medals on it.

"Hello, Rainey," Leilani said warmly to me. "I'm so glad you could come."

Awak came around his desk, and walked over to me. "Mr. Rainey! What a pleasure to have you here this afternoon!"

Leilani's father was rather short and thin, and looked unhealthy to me. He wore rimless glasses that gave him a professional look. He had in fact been a professor, in Hawaii and here in Samoa, before going into politics, and had written a book on the history of Samoa. His face was thin, his hair thinning, and his complexion had a sallow, yellow cast to it. He was wearing a formal suit of western clothes, as was the other man not in uniform.

"I'm pleased to meet you, Dr. Awak," I said to him. I looked around. "I wasn't aware that this meeting was going to be such an . . . enlarged one."

"Ah, I'm sorry if we misled you," he apologized. "But I felt it was imperative that Mr. Mataafa and General Tofa were here. Mataafa is our Deputy Prime Minister, and the general is in charge of both the new Civil Guard and our police force."

I looked them over, and they sized me up. Mataafa was a man who obviously had some blood in him other than Samoan, and looked more like a desert bandit than a politician in the South Pacific. He had a smell of decadence about him that was obvious. He was fat, oily, and aloof-looking, and I disliked him more on first sight than I had Mannheim. General Tofa was big for a Samoan, also overweight, but seemingly a tough guy. His eyes were diamond-hard in a broad, pockmarked face, and he looked at me now in a very hostile way. His dark hair was also thinning, and he wore it slicked down hard onto his oily head.

"Mr. Rainey," Mataafa said with a hard smile, offering his hand.

I took it, and did not like the soft feel of it. I nodded. Then Tofa extended his hand, and it was a harder one. "We've all heard a lot about you, Rainey," he said, not smiling.

I glanced toward Leilani. "I didn't know that," I said.

"Oh, my daughter has done quite some research on you, Mr. Rainey," Awak said, still smiling the weak, unhealthy smile. "You have an impressive record across the world."

"It's just another way to make a living," I told him.

Awak seated us all around the desk. All except Leilani, who sent and stood behind him, leaning on the wall there. She probably wanted to remind all present that she was Awak's daughter, and as such a very powerful force in Samoa. She now wore a lemon-hued, wispy dress, her dark hair put up on her head, little ringlets of it beside her face. I was reminded of the night before, and wondered how many other times she had used her sex to get what she wanted, in this small seat of power.

"Now," Awak said, clasping his hands before him on the desk. "I understand you have refused to consider a contract to . . . eliminate Fredrik Mannheim from Samoa, Mr. Rainey."

"That's right," I told him.

"Quite frankly, that surprises us," Mataafa put in. He had lit a cigarette and stuck it in a long, ivory holder. "We were sure that a man like you would have no scruples against such an assignment."

Awak gave Mataafa a hard look. General Tofa seemed pleased with Mataafa's remark, and smiled a brittle smile.

"Why don't you just speak for yourself, Minister?" Leilani said coldly, obviously irritated by Mataafa.

Mataafa glanced at her and shrugged. "I say what I feel."

While they all watched, I got out a Cuban cigar and lit it. It was the only smoking I did, and I could not get them often. I blew a perfect smoke ring toward the high ceiling. "It's not a matter of scruples, Mataafa," I said easily. "It's just a job I'd prefer not to obligate myself to. I don't think it's possible."

Tofa grunted. "Ah, a defeatist mercenary. An interesting combination, Rainey."

I was getting it from both Mataafa and Tofa, and it was clear that they had both opposed my being hired. It had been Awak's and Leilani's idea, and they had found Colonel Tupua to go along with them. But Tofa was Tupua's boss, and although it was clear that Tupua was upset with Tofa and Mataafa too, he now kept his silence.

"Not defeatist, General," I said, studying his hard face. "Just realistic. If you think Mannheim is so easy to kill, why don't you go do the job yourself?"

Tofa's broad, fat face clouded over like an angry sea before a typhoon. He obviously disliked the very idea of my being there. "I have more important matters to handle in the affairs of this fledgling society than to play adventurer against a rebel," he lectured me. "You do not send a general to do a private soldier's work, and it is presumptuous of you to suggest it."

"If this were work for a private soldier, General, you'd have sent one to get it done," I said sourly. "And I had the idea that there's nothing more important to you at this time than to rid yourself of Fredrik Mannhaim. Surely a general might go, to save these islands from tyranny?"

Tofa rose dark-faced from the chair he was seated on. "You are an impudent upstart nobody, damn you! A greedy hireling who kills for money, yet too cowardly to take on a job where there might be some personal danger to you!" He turned to Awak. "I told you as much when you suggested this absurd scheme!"

Tupua rose also. "Colonel Rainey is not greedy, General. Nor is there any record of cowardice in his background."

Tofa spun on him. "Sit down, Colonel! You are out of line!"

Tupua hesitated, then took his seat again.

"Tupua speaks the truth, General," Leilani put in.

"Rainey has a fine record behind him. That's why we went to him."

Tofa glared at Leilani, then at Awak. "Are you going to continue to allow this girl and military inferiors to influence your decisions of state? If so, it is surely time you stepped down and allowed someone in better health to run this government, Minister?"

"So you can take his place, General?" Leilani said loudly.

The thing was getting out of hand. Awak rose from behind the desk with dignity, and looked taller than he was. "All right, let's attempt to keep some semblance of order here, gentlemen. We did not call Mr. Rainey here to reveal our many internal differences."

I was impressed with Awak's cool. But he did look sick, there was no doubt about it. I had heard that he had a lung disease, probably TB, and that he had not treated it properly.

"As for my state of health, General," Awak went on, "and my reliance on persons close to me for counsel, I believe those are matters that are my own private business, at this time."

Tofa gave Awak a hard look, then turned away. "We have been through all this before," he said angrily.

"Perhaps we should wait to discuss these internal matters," Mataafa put in nicely, "until this outsider has been dismissed." He nodded toward me.

Leilani came out into the center of the room, looking beautiful. There was a big window on the end wall of the office, and sunlight came from there and made her dress a brighter yellow. "You two amaze me!" she said loudly. "The colonel and I go to great lengths to bring this man here who could possibly help us in our fight against lawlessness and rebellion, and all you can do is insult him! I am ashamed to be a part of this!"

"Please, daughter," Awak said quietly. "Go down to the police chief and set up that appointment he requested earlier. We don't need you here at the moment."

Leilani looked over at him, understanding he wanted to spare her any further trouble. "All right," she said reluctantly. She turned to me. "I'll see you after this is finished, Rainey."

I smiled at her. "I'll look forward to it," I said.

Leilani left, and Tofa watched her go. When the door was closed behind her, he turned to me. "If you have no interest in Dr. Awak's offer, why are you here?"

I shrugged. "I promised Leilani I would hear you out."

He made a low sound in his throat, and turned to Awak. "I say let him go. It was a bad idea from the start, even Rainey agrees with that. We can deal with Mannheim."

"The way you've dealt with him up to now?" Awak suggested.

Tofa gave Awak a searing look. "We have contained his force in the area of the west of the island. We caught a patrol of his and wiped them out, remember?"

"Mannheim has occupied three villages with his troops," Tupua intervened. "He has defeated two of our Guard garrisons. He is recruiting new troops every day—hooligans, murderers, and other scum who have no hesitation in killing innocent people. Very soon he may make a move on the capital here. Will we be ready to stop him?"

"The Civil Guard will do its duty, Tupua. Despite a cadre of passimists like yourself."

"I say we can't settle for containment," Tupua said in a firm voice. "We must do something about Mannheim now, before it is too late for us."

"I concur with that," Awak said.

Mataafa made a face. Between him and Tofa, he was the most offensive because of his personal slovenliness. "I don't see what all the fuss is about. We still bring in taxes, don't we? We still live well, we in government. The people will always have their poverty and their crime and their multitude of complaints. Can we ever really change that? The important thing is that they have us to look over them. To throw them scraps from the table, and keep some order amo them when they fall to fighting among themselves."

I couldn't believe the callousness of the bastard. I'm not a crusader myself, but people like Mataafa always amaze me with their complete indifference to the welfare of the world.

"For God's sake, Mataafa," Awak said heavily. "Do you realize how you sound?"

Mataafa shrugged. "I am a realist," he said. "Like the general here."

Tofa looked toward Mataafa with disgust. He was a strong man, Mataafa a weak one. Tofa had no interest in having Mataafa as an ally. "As the lady pointed out earlier, Mataafa," he said acidly, "you must remember to speak only for yourself."

Mataafa gave him a hurt look, as if he had been

betrayed by a friend. But it was clear that Tofa did not want this half-breed minister as a friend. Tupua glanced at me knowingly.

Awak sighed. "Let's return to the subject at hand. Mr. Rainey, how would you feel about the proposal if we offered you more money?"

Tofa glared toward Awak. "What? More money? Have you suddenly lost all judgment, for God's sake?"

Awak ignored him. "Well, Mr. Rainey?"

I shook my head. "The offer made to me was very generous, Dr. Awak. It isn't the money. I didn't like the idea when I came here, and I like it even less, now that I've met these two." I motioned toward Mataafa and Tofa, and Mataafa's face darkened with renewed hostility. "I have to have some respect for the people I work for."

Tupua grinned slightly. Tofa looked like he wanted to shoot me right there on the spot, or throw me out the sunlit window. "You go too far, damn you!"

Mataafa turned indolently toward Awak. "Get rid of him," he said. "He isn't up to our standards, Minister."

I rose, and Tupua did too, watching me. "On the contrary," I said. "You're not up to mine, Mataafa. I'm on my way, Dr. Awak. I think this meeting was a mistake."

"Rainey, please," Tupua said.

Awak came closer to me. "Yes, wait, Mr. Rainey." He turned to Tofa. "General, you and Mataafa have expressed your positions clearly in this matter. We'll talk further about it later. Now, however, I would like to have a few minutes with Rainey alone."

Tofa frowned suspiciously at Awak. "As you wish," he finally said in the hard voice.

He and Mataafa left quickly, and Tupua followed them. Awak and I were at last alone, the way I had thought we would be from the beginning.

"Nice people you're associated with," I said.

Awak sighed. "General Tofa has opposed me from the moment I took office, in one way or another. I was forced to take Mataafa into my cabinet, by the powerful *matai.* It was a compromise that allowed me to take office, Mr. Rainey."

"It's not far different in my country," I admitted.

He smiled at me. "Please sit down and give me a small additional moment with you."

I took my seat again, and Awak sat on the corner of his long mahogany desk. I glanced around the room, at its rich paneling, its thick carpet, its paintings on the walls. A Samoan flag stood in a corner behind his desk. I wondered if Mannheim had a different one in mind.

"I frankly don't care what Mataafa and Tofa want," Awak told me now. "I brought them in so they couldn't accuse me of doing this behind their backs, later."

"I've heard some things about Mataafa," I said. "That he takes money under the table for favors. That he abuses his tax-collecting authority. That he has a large Swiss bank account."

Awak nodded heavily. "I do what I can, Mr. Rainey, to curb abuses of authority here in Western Samoa. It is the platform on which I ran for office.

But things seem to have run downhill since my illness. I have a lung congestion that won't go away, it seems." He took a handkerchief out, and coughed lightly into it. "I'm not the same man who took office a while ago. And my enemies take advantage of that fact. Now there is Mannheim. Nobody takes him seriously, it seems, but myself and a few close to me."

"I'd take him seriously," I said. "I think he'll be here in Apia if you don't do something about him soon."

"And yet you won't help us," he commented.

"I won't take on an impossible job," I corrected him. Actually, I had grown an interest in Mannheim and Western Samoa since the meeting with Leilani and Tupua. And my interest was further heightened by the general and Mataafa. Awak needed me more than he realized. It was clear to me, if not to him, that Mannheim was not the only danger to Awak's stable authority in Samoa. "But I didn't say I wouldn't help you, Dr. Awak."

His expression changed. "What are you saying, Mr. Rainey?"

I settled back in my chair. I stuck the cigar back into my mouth and puffed on it to renew it, then pulled it back out. "Mannheim can't be very easily assassinated. But he can be beaten. In the field. If you had somebody with some military skill who really wanted to beat him."

"Are you making me an offer?" Awak asked with a slow smile.

"This is an interesting problem, for a soldier," I admitted. "The terrain would be a lot like I've encountered in Ecuador. The military situation is similar, too. What kinds of weapons do your Civil Guard have?"

He shook his head. "Inadequate ones, I'm afraid. General Tofa has always assured me that they are sufficient. Old American rifles, some Brazilian handguns. A cannon left by the British in World War II."

"Great," I said. "Are you aware that Mannheim is buying the most sophisticated weapons he can het his hands on? Automatic rifles, rocket mortars, anti-tank weapons?"

"I have heard many rumors," he said. "But did not wish to believe them. It's my sickness, Mr. Rainey. I'm afraid I've not been a very strong leader in this past year."

"You need weapons," I said. "You need somebody to train your troops in guerrilla warfare. And most important, you need someone to lead them who knows how to win."

"And that someone," he said. "It could possibly be you, Mr. Rainey?"

I sat there thinking. There was a couple of mercs in the area I might be able to hire as lieutenants under my command. And Tupua seemed a competent military leader. That would be a start. There would undoubtedly be others who could be trusted to fight when a fight came with Mannheim.

I got up and put the cigar out in a tray on Awak's desk, and turned to him, standing beside him. "I'd be willing to take command of a special force of your Guard—it might require almost the entire strength you have—and go after Mannheim before he comes after you. And I'd do it for half of what you offered me for an assassination. A hundred grand, no guarantees on my part. Additional funds to hire some other mercenaries if they're needed. The whole thing, with weaponry thrown in, won't cost any more than you offered me to kill Mannheim, if we win. If we lose, well, you would have lost anyway."

He nodded. "That sounds like a very reasonable offer, Mr. Rainey. And one that pleases me more than you can imagine. I would personally prefer to meet Mannheim out in the open and defeat him honorably than kill him in his bed, anyway."

"If you win this way, Mannheim will probably die in battle," I suggested. "Or you can put him in one of your prisons for the rest of his life, or execute him under the law."

"Then you will accept a commission in the Civil Guard?" Awak asked me.

I nodded. "A temporary one of colonel should give me enough authority to get the job done. Is that okay with you?"

"It is perfect," Awak said.

"I don't want Tofa second-guessing me, though. I want autonomy in this defense project, answerable only to you."

"You have it," he said. "I will put the necessary papers through this afternoon, and you will be sworn in and given a uniform."

"Sounds fine," I said. "I intend to return to Pago Pago to do some immediate recruiting the first thing."

"General Tofa is not going to like this," Awak said. "You will have to stand up against him and his hostility, Colonel Rainey."

The mention of rank did not escape me. "I know

that. I'd like to have your permission to investigate the general."

His brow creased. "Investigate him?"

"Just a notion of mine. Do you object?"

He hesitated. "No," he said. "I don't."

"I'll be in touch with you after I'm sworn in," I said.

"Excellent, Colonel Rainey. Believe me, I'm relieved to have you aboard."

When I left Awak's office, there was a Guard officer standing out in the corridor, watching me leave. I figured it was one of Tofa's personal spies, but I doubted that he had heard anything in Awak's office. I saw him again downstairs later, when I was going through the paperwork of signing into the Guard. He had apparently been assigned to keep an eye on me. I didn't mind. I was going to keep an eye on Tofa too. I had already formed some pretty definite ideas about the general that I wanted to check out.

When I got back to the hotel that afternoon I already had a call from Leilani Awak, and she had left a message for me to call her back at her home, which was the Awak ministerial residence. I ignored the note for the time being. I did not want to be distracted by anything personal. I was now heading into something that could mean life or death for me and a lot of others, and I had things to do. In one of my long bullshit conversations with John Boy at Pago Pago, he had mentioned talking with a guy in Apia who professed to have information against certain elements of Awak's government. His name was Chiang Ching and he was from Taiwan. He had holed up in a fleabag hotel on the waterfront, John Boy had told me, and had tried to sell John Boy information about one of Awak's lesser ministers.

I ate an early evening meal at the hotel and it left a lump in my gut. There are some places you hire on to fight where the chow and accommodations are first class, and that eases the discomforts of those little wars. Samoa was not one of those places. Also, I knew that out there in those hills where the fighting would occur were many kinds of tropical terrors worse than bedbugs. I've often thought that the best place to fight a war, if you could take the cold, would be Antarctica. At least, when you got a fire built under you, you would be able to sleep undisturbed. Not so in the tropics.

It was dark out when I walked down to the waterfront hotel. It was a real dump, a lot worse than the one I had chosen for myself. It was a narrow, three-story building that looked like it had been there for about a thousand years. On one side of it squatted a lower building that housed a tattoo parlor where opium could be obtained, and on the other was a rowdy-looking saloon. Sailors from Argentina had clustered outside the bar and were ogling two prostitutions down the street about thirty yards. There was a lot of loud music and yelling from the saloon.

I went into the hotel and wrinkled my nose at some ugly odor. I figured it was the proprietor's meal cooking, mixed in with some other smells I didn't want to bother to analyze. A scruffy-looking Samoan told me I could find Chiang Ching on the second floor in Room 205, and I climbed a dirty stairway up there. There was plaster hanging from the corridor walls, and graffiti everywhere. I knocked lightly on the door of 205 and waited. A moment later it opened and the Taiwanese stood there.

He was tiny, with spindly legs sticking awkwardly from khaki shorts, and he wore a dirty body shirt. Black hair hung onto his forehead. He was a rather young man, but his face was prematurely aged. He looked up at me with his head cocked and eyes squinted down.

"Heh? Yes?"

"Are you Chiang Ching?" I asked him.

He looked me over. "You are American?"

"Yeah. American. Can we talk a few minutes? Inside?"

He hesitated, shrugged. "Okay, Joe."

I followed him back into the room. It was awful. There was litter everywhere, more than on the streets outside. Beer bottles, newspapers, remains of food. He seated me on a straight chair that creaked under my weight and threatened to collapse completely. I looked around some more. There was a low, unmade bed, a table with more litter on it, and an outdated calender hanging on a wall by a nail. The place was depressing. I wondered how a man who lived like this could possibly be any use to me.

"I hear you sometimes have information to sell," I said to him. He stood near me, studying me closely. He had gotten a marijuana cigarette from somewhere and was inhaling on it. "Information about the present government in Apia."

He nodded slowly. "I know many persons in government, persons who hear things others don't," he said in an accented, sing-song voice. His dark eyes were narrowly slitted, his nose broad. He looked very Oriental.

"Do you hear anything about General Tofa?" I said. "Or Deputy Minister Mataafa?"

His face changed, and a half-smile crossed it briefly and was gone, like the shadow of an Asian vulture. "Ah. You are interested in the big guns, I see. What kind of information do you want, American?"

I shrugged slightly. "Anything you can tell me, I guess." I reached into a pocket and offered him a wad of Samoan dollars. He took them and counted them slowly, and looked unimpressed. He went and slumped onto the bed.

"Mataafa is a typical opportunist politician here," he began. "He has no interest in the people, only in lining his pockets. His evil is an omission rather than commission, if you follow me. He doesn't have people killed or arrested. He has no contact with the people at all. He parties, drinks, and collects money for his own personal enrichment. That is what he thinks the office is for. Of course, if a person like Mannheim gained power, Mataafa would join him without hesitation, and then would become a greater evil than he presently is."

I was impressed with the understanding of this Chinese who had seemed to have given up on life. "What about Tofa?" I asked.

"Ah, now that is another matter," Chiang Ching explained, leaning forward toward me suddenly. "The general has disposed of citizens that Dr. Awak doesn't even know about. And badly abused others.

He tolerates no opposition to him. There is a rumor that just started recently about him."

He stopped to inhale the reefer, and I waited impatiently. "Yes?" I urged him on.

"It is said that Tofa has made a deal with Mannheim," Chiang said easily.

I nodded to myself. My instincts about Tofa made me believe in the truth of the rumor. "Can you prove or disprove that?" I said to him.

He made a face. "I have made no such effort. Tofa is well protected by his underlings in the Civil Guard and police. But there is a retired colonel."

"What retired colonel?"

"A fellow named Matautu. He left the service of his new country early because he did not want to work under Tofa. It is said that Tofa considers him a political enemy. Matautu still lives here in Apia, in one of the outlying districts. He might be able to give you something on Tofa. He asked to have a private interview with Dr. Awak recently, but then cancelled out. Awak never pursued it."

"The prime minister should be replaced," I said. "He isn't physically capable of performing his governmental duties."

Chiang grinned. "Now you are talking like Mannheim," he said.

I rose. "Not quite," I corrected him. I gave him another small wad of bills. "Thanks for talking with me. If you learn anything specific about Tofa, call me at the Upolu House. I'll make it worth your time."

"I'll keep that in mind, Mr.—"

"Rainey," I said. "Starting today, it's Colonel

Rainey. Of the Western Samoa Civil Guard."

When I left, Chiang Ching was staring after me quizzically, as if it was me that was planning an overthrow of the government.

When I got back out onto the street, I got the feeling immediately that I was being watched, and I remembered the guard at Government House who had been waiting outside in the corridor after my private talk with Awak. I looked around, though, and couldn't see him anywhere. I convinced myself that I was imagining things, and looked for a taxi and couldn't find one. I started walking back to the Upolu House.

I hadn't gotten more than a couple blocks from the fleabag hotel on the waterfront when I encountered the trouble I had sensed at the moment I had left the building.

I passed an alleyway that was dark and forbidding, with no one else around, when the figure stepped out in front of me. He was a burly Samoan, one of those many who hung out on the streets and mugged tourists and terrorized locals. He was my height, with a thick, muscular frame and an ugly face. He wore a gold earring in his right ear, but that did not in any way make him look effeminate. He held a thin wooden club in his left hand.

"Where you been, Mr. Rainey?" he said in good English. But the way he said it made my flesh crawl.

I started to reply, when another figure separated itself from the shadows of the alley, and came around to my other side. This guy was slim and wiry but looked as tough as the first one. He was a half-breed of some kind, with some Oriental in him. He looked grubby, like a user. This one wielded a stiletto in his right hand, and he wasn't disposed to talk to me.

I looked into the shadows, and that appeared to be all of them. It was enough. I turned back to the burly guy. "Is that any of your business?" I said carefully. "You don't look like you're with the police."

"No, we're not the police." He grinned. "But we know where you went, anyway. You're snooping, Rainey. You're looking for trouble. Now you found it."

A car drove past slowly, and I could see a man and woman inside. They looked at us, and then quickly turned away and drove on. They were used to muggings here, and didn't want to get involved.

"I've got no quarrel with you two," I said. "Now get the hell out of my way."

I started to move past them, and the guy with the knife moved out to stop me. I hesitated, then came on past him.

He made a lightning-quick thrust with the knife, toward my ribs. I sidestepped the thrust and he came on, off-balance. I swung the back of my hand into the side of his head, and he yelled and went flying off his feet, hitting the pavement near me. When I turned back to the other guy, the burly one, the club was already descending vicioiusly. I partially deflected it, but it connected on the back of my neck and my shoulder, and I felt needles of pain rocket through me. I punched stiffened fingers into his face, and one caught him in the left eyeball, damaging the eye immediately. Another yell as he staggered past me.

The stiletto man was back on his feet, and furious,

his eyes wild. He glanced toward his buddy, who was holding his hand up to his lacerated eye and yelling. Stiletto hurled the knife hand at me, and got lucky and cut me across the forearm. I looked down and saw blood run down into the palm of my hand, and something burst into my chest from my inner gut like a wild animal. I had been going to defend myself only, intent merely on chasing off or injuring my attackers. But now everything was different, as it had so often been different on the battlegrounds of the world for me.

I did a complete pirouette turn, coming back around with my hand slamming into the face of the knife-carrier. My hand connected with the bridge of his nose, and there was a sharp cracking sound there as bone snapped loudly, was splintered, and went exploding back into his brain like sharp darts, cutting and slicing through his head. He went running backwards, the knife thrown at a building wall, his eyes saucered white, a scream beginning in his throat. He followed the knife against the wall, and when he crashed into it the scream was shut off as if a radio had been turned off suddenly. He fell to the pavement then and began thrashing wildly there, already dead.

When I spun back to the half-blind guy, I found him somewhat recovered from the eye gouge and trying to put me down a final time. He was swinging the club again, this time like he wanted to crush my skull with it.

"You bastard! You bastard!" he was saying deep in his throat, in a kind of whine.

This time I was ready for him. I ducked the wild swing and it only grazed my already aching shoulder. He stumbled past me. I chopped into his ribs and three of them cracked under the impact. He went into a rolling fall to the pavement. I stepped over him, that thing still up in my chest, and kicked him alongside the head. Another cracking sound, and it was over. A shudder rippled through his thick body, and crimson began worming out through his nose, ears, and mouth.

I stood there breathing shallowly, letting the thing inside me crawl down where it belonged. It was what an officer in Nam had once called the Neanderthal Instinct, the thing that helped soldiers survive against a deadly enemy. Most of us that fought for a living had it. I looked down at the pavement. Death was usually the result when you sent amateurs against a pro. I could have told them that, but they wouldn't have listened. Now they had paid the price.

I wrapped a handkerchief around my forearm to stop the bleeding. My head was beginning to ache along with my neck and shoulder. But the wound was shallow and the headache would be gone tomorrow. For those jerks on the pavement, there would be no tomorrow.

I would lose no sleep over them.

THREE

The next morning I moved out of the Upolu House and into a Bachelor Officers Quarters building not far from the central square of Apia, and only a half-mile from Government House. Awak had cleared out a nice little apartment for me on the top floor that was all white-washed walls, arched doorways, and glass windows overlooking the town and the port. It was already furnished with heavy, Spanish-type furniture and thick carpets, and even a bar that was stocked with Johnny Walker and other tasty spirits. I kind of liked it. If I had been there as a vacationer, I might have stayed in the place for quite some time. But I rarely took a vacation as such anywhere. There was always work for a guy like me, if I wanted it. And I did.

Before noon, an orderly in a starched khaki uniform delivered some boxes to me. There were uniforms, polished boots, sidearms. I put on a green uniform and it surprisingly fit, as did the boots. Awak was taking good care of me. I took the medals off the jacket of the uniform, and then decided I wouldn't be wearing the jacket anyway. I put the insignia on the green shirt, tucked the peaked cap under my arm, and left the place looking more like a West-Pointer than a merc. I didn't mind. I had found out that a nice uniform brings respect to its wearer, whether the respect is deserved or not. So maybe I'd get along in Apia better if I was accepted for the uniform I was wearing. I was obviously going to need all the help I could get.

In early afternoon I had another private conference with Awak, and he was very pleased to see me in his country's uniform. I reminded him that my commission was temporary, as was my stay in Samoa. He asked me to take over training of the troops immediately, and I agreed. I told him I would take command of the Apia garrison the very next day, and it would be the core of my army that would be used against Mannheim.

Later in the day I returned to Pago Pago, to look up John Boy. It was dark when I returned to the saloon where we had had those long evening bull-sessions, and John Boy was there, on his third brandy. He loved brandy, and got a little disgruntled when he couldn't get hold of any.

"Well, I'll be damned," he said when I sat down at his table. "I thought maybe you're returned to L.A. without saying your farewells, Rainey."

"No, I'm not going to the States just yet," I said. "Let me order you a whisky."

"No, I'm not drinking tonight," I told him.

John Boy frowned an All-American frown. "Does that mean you're working?" he said.

I nodded. "I took a job in Apia."

The light blue eyes narrowed down on me. "No shit!"

"Dr. Awak was very persuasive," I grinned. "I'm going to train his little army to fight Mannheim."

He grunted. "You picked the wrong side, Rainey."

"Maybe. But it's the side I feel comfortable on. What about you?"

"What about me?"

"Wouldn't you like it some to show Fredrik Mannheim he isn't the little god he seems to think he is? For good pay?"

"Mannheim would pay me more," he said.

"But you'd be fighting under my command," I said. "If you joined his army of muggers and cutthroats, you'd be going against me. And I'm such a much nicer guy than that Kraut." I grinned at him.

He returned it. "Yeah, maybe you're right, Rainey. I didn't much like that bastard when we met him. Or the fact that he's got Rabbit Burroughs killing for him."

"Well, then," I said.

He seemed to notice my green uniform for the first time, and the eagles on my shoulders. "Is that the uniform?"

"That is it."

"Nice," he said. "I always liked a nice uniform."

"That used to be a deciding factor for Crazy Jake," I told him.

"He's here."

"Who? Jake?"

He nodded. "He was here in the bar the other night. He was with some Samoan whore. He said he'd just joined up with Mannheim. Wanted me to do the same."

"Oh, Christ," I said.

"He's been holed up out on the beach since then, drinking and screwing. Remember how much he liked those Zulu girls?"

I gave him a small grin. "Yeah, I remember. Where is he on the beach?"

"I'm not sure, but I think I could find it."

I leaned foward. "Listen, John Boy. Uniform or no uniform, this is going to be your kind of fight, on this side of it. The way things stand at this moment, the Civil Guard and all established authority in Western Samoa are the underdogs. Mannheim has the momentum, and a clear expectation of winning. Our troops are untrained, unarmed kids, some of them already looking up to Mannheim as some kind of goddamn hero. We'll have to kick them out on their asses, the ones that aren't solidly in our camp. It's a big, uphill job, the kind you always told me you liked. If we win against Mannheim, you could go down in Samoan history as a goddamn saint."

"And if we lose?" he said.

"They may bury us in a Samoan grave," I admitted. "But you always knew you might not go in bed at home."

John Boy sighed, and ran a hand through his blond-streaked hair. "Hell, okay, Rainey. I'm on your team. What's my rank in this latest war?"

"Captain," I said. "Directly under my command."

"Just like Namibia," he suggested.

"Just like it."

"Like you said, it sounds comfortable."

"Don't get too comfortable," I advised. "We've got some tough days ahead of us. Now, do you think we can find that beach place of Crazy Jake's?"

"Let's give it a try," he said.

It was not much of a drive to the rented shack on the beach that Crazy Jake had mentioned to John Boy in passing. We parked John Boy's Hertz car at the end of a beach road, walked for maybe a half-mile, and found the place on an isolated strand. There were lights burning so I figured Jake was at home—his temporary home-away-from-home. Or should I say, home away from the States? Most of us no longer had any real home back there. That was the way it was with most mercs.

I banged on the door and got no reply, so we just walked into the place. It was all bamboo and rattan, with shutters that swung outward on hinges and no screens on the windows. It was a two-room shack with a thatched roof, and one of the rooms was a grubby bath. Jake was zonked out on a bed in a far corner.

"Hey, Jake!" I yelled. "You got company!"

The big man on the bed was startled awake. Suddenly his right hand came up with a revolver in it, and the sonofabitch began firing wildly in our direction.

"*Down!*" I yelled at John Boy.

We both hit the wood-plank floor near the door. There were bright explosions from the thick revolver that banged on our eardrums, and hot lead flew around us, chewing up bamboo and wood and shattering a bottle of rum sitting on a nearby table.

The clamor of gunfire was raucous in the enclosed space.

"Jake! It's us, Rainey and John Boy!"

"We're under attack! Kill the goddamn bastards! Take no frigging prisoners!"

"Stop it, Jake!" John Boy yelled. He had drawn the Walther P-38 automatic he always carried on him, ready to kill Jake if he had to. *"It's only us!"*

Crazy Jake's eyes changed, and a wild thing seemed to ebb out of them. He dropped the gun to his side and focused on us. He was naked except for a pair of boxer shorts. He swung his legs off the bed, and stared at me for a long moment.

"Jim Rainey?" he said in a deep, thick voice.

"The same, Jake," I answered.

We got up off the floor, and John Boy returned the automatic to his tunic. He went and slumped on a straight chair, and I walked over to Jake and heaved myself onto the bed beside him.

"Shit," he said thickly, the alcohol still in him. "Don't ever come up on a man like that, Rainey. You're liable to get your frigging head blown off." He was a tanned, muscular, ropy guy with a face that you would not want to meet in a dark alley. His hair and eyes were dark, and I knew that he had a mixture of Italian and Irish in him. But the blood that gave him his crazy moods was the Apache he had inherited from a grandfather. His torso was laced with scars, and his face had a long one from left eye to cheek, put there by a frenzied African in the heat of battle.

"We didn't mean to surprise you, Jake," John Boy told him.

Crazy Jake wiped a big hand across his face. The gun he was still holding was a Webley Mark IV .38, a British-made weapon from the same period as John Boy's Walther. The Mark IV had been used by the Commandos against the Nazis, so between them Jake and John Boy had the Big War pretty well covered. A lot of mercs prefered period firearms to the most modern ones, because they felt they were better designed and constructed.

"Don't ever come up on me like that," Jake repeated.

"I heard you were shacking up, Jake," I said. "Where's the girl?"

He looked over at me. "You never look any different, for Christ's sake," he said. "The rest of us get older and uglier, and you just go on looking the same, Rainey. You got a painting of yourself in a goddamn footlocker somewhere that would scare little kids?"

I laughed. I had always liked Jake Murphy, as much as you can like a crazy, ornery bastard like him. In Nam, he had volunteered for patrol after patrol, just to get to kill more Cong. He had developed his own methods of killing—some of which were imaginative, to say the least. It was said that he killed a Cong once with an eagle's feather. I never asked how. We all had our little specialties. Crazy Jake just had a few more, and many were bizarre.

"I just live right, Jake," I told him. "Good food, good booze, good company."

"I got rid of the Samoan whore," he said, stretching. "I got sick of the smell of fried bananas around here." He gestured toward an old wood stove in a corner. "Can you imagine, fried bananas?"

"They're big in Latin America too," I told him. "John Boy here tells me you signed up with Mannheim."

Crazy Jake glanced at John Boy. "Yeah. Got a good offer, Rainey. You and the kid ought to do the same. Mannheim's gonna own these goddamn islands in a few weeks."

"Not if I can help it," I said.

"Huh?" He stuck a fat cigar into his mouth, a cheapie in comparison to the kind I preferred. He did not light it, but just chewed on it. I had never actually seen him smoke one.

"I've just been hired by the government in Apia," I said. "To bust Mannheim's balls."

Crazy Jake squinted down at me. "Well, kiss my ass and call me a fairy," he growled. "It looks like you and me will finally be shooting at each other, Rainey."

"John Boy joined up too," I said.

Jake looked at him. "With Awak and Tofa and that bunch of jerks?" he said to John Boy.

John Boy shrugged. "I'd rather fight with Rainey than Rabbit Burroughs."

"Shit, Rabbit's a nobody with Mannheim," Jake argued.

"What about Mueller?" I said.

"I don't have to like Mueller to get along with him."

"Will you be at equal rank with him?" I asked.

He hesitated. "Well, no. Mannheim gave him colonel rank."

"That could cause you trouble," I said. "You know what Mueller is like. He's a goddamn bastard, chicken-shit all the way to his polished boots."

"Tell me about it," he said. "I know that frigging Afrikaaner better than you, Rainey. Did you know that he once screwed a female corpse in the mouth, for God's sake? The man is an animal."

John Boy and I exchanged glances, and he smiled slightly. To hear Crazy Jake Murphy talking about another merc being an animal was a little humorous.

"You want to work under somebody like him?" I said.

Jake looked at me. "It's good pay, Rainey."

"John Boy said the same. But even if we can't quite match it, you'll enjoy the war on our side of it. I don't think you will much, on the other side."

Jake sighed. He was sober-looking now. "Maybe. But I already took an advance from them, for Christ's sake. I don't want to owe a guy like Mannheim."

"You wouldn't," I said. "You can never owe a guy like Mannheim. But if you wanted to, I'd find a way of sending the advance back over to him."

He made a face, and it was an ugly one. "Why didn't you come around a couple of days ago?" he said.

"I was busy deciding whether to get involved in this at all," I said to him. "If you come with us, you'll be ranked at captain, like John Boy here. We can use your expertise with explosives and field pieces. John Boy will train in small arms and tactical maneuvers."

"You sound like we're at Fort Benning, for Christ's sake," Jake said acidly. "You think you can teach these coconut-eaters how to enfilade or fire a field piece?"

"We have the same people to work with as Mannheim," I said.

He grunted deeply. "Except he's already creamed off the tough ones. The ex-cons and hoodlums. The rest of them are farmers and clerks, Rainey."

"It was farmers and clerks that won the big one against Hitler's elite," I reminded him.

"They had something to fight for they believed in," he told me. "What do you have, Rainey?"

"That depends on what you give me," I said.

Jake thought that over, and finally he set the revolver on the table next to the bed, as if he had remembered it for the first time since the shooting. "Sorry I blasted away when you came in. I was dead asleep when you yelled my name. I thought I was in Lebanon."

"No sweat," John Boy told him.

Jake grimaced. "Hell, what's the difference? You want me, I'll go with you. I'm not going to ever get rich at this anyway."

"I'm glad you're coming aboard, Jake," I said.

He looked at me under heavy brows and grinned. "Mannheim did promise me Chief of Police in his new Samoan State, though," he grinned. "The chief of the whole goddamn police."

"You were never cut out to be a policeman, Jake," I suggested.

"You don't have to tell me that, Rainey. I've got it in my head that policemen are the enemy. I guess it's because I've spent so much time behind their bars at one time or another. No, I won't miss that job at all."

"Then it's settled," I said. "Can you both return to Apia with me tonight?"

"What have we got better to do?" John Boy said.

Jake rose from the bed and stuck the revolver in the waistband of his undershorts. "Let's go stick it up Mannheim's ass," he said in that growl of his.

I couldn't have said it better.

FOUR

It was the next morning that I had yet another meeting with Dr. Awak. He had had another coughing attack during the night, and was looking very pale and worn out when we met again in his office. Leilani was there too, and we met in the outer office before going in to see her father. She asked why I hadn't called her, and I explained the trip to Pago Pago. She did not seem pleased with my explanation.

At a little after ten the three of us were seated in Awak's office. Leilani got him a rum drink from the bar not far from his desk, and offered me a drink. I said no. Awak reclined on his leather chair.

"I invited General Tofa to this meeting," he told me in a weaker voice than before, "and also Mataafa. They both declined. Tofa has expressed extreme displeasure with your commission in the Civil Guard, threatening to resign. He won't, of course."

"I don't trust him," I said.

Awak frowned at me. "I know you've had your differences with him in your brief encounter. But surely you think you can work with him, Colonel Rainey?"

For the occasion, I was wearing the dress jacket of the Civil Guard . . . a tie—the whole works. Everything except the medals they had given me for actions against Mannheim I had never been in. I looked like a Bolivian general sitting there with my gold-braid cap on my knee.

"Tofa could be dangerous to you, Dr. Awak. I'd like your permission to check him out on a more formal basis."

"Dangerous?" Leilani said. Her hair was down long, with spit curls at the sides of her face. She was wearing a sheer blouse tucked into form-fitting pants and she looked good enough to eat. "Really?"

"Oh, please, Colonel Rainey," Awak smiled. "Let's not you become as paranoid as the general himself. I don't think Tofa has it in him to challenge my authority here. He isn't the type."

"Do you really know what type he is?" I wondered.

Awak looked nettled. "I think we must concentrate on getting an army trained and ready to fight, Rainey. We have little time for intrigue among us. Don't worry, I can handle General Tofa."

I let it drop. But I knew that Awak had as much chance of handling Tofa as a *novillero* would have with a fighting bull that has been released from the kill to fight a second time in the arena.

"All right, Minister," I said. "But I was hoping Tofa would be here to meet my new recruits."

"Ah, you've hired subordinates?" Awak asked.

I nodded. "It happened that two men I've fought with were in Pago Pago. Professional soldiers. Experts in warfare, Minister. I've offered them special captain's pay for the duration. Believe me, it's money well spent."

Awak did not look convinced. "Yes, I suppose so. As long as you can control them, Rainey."

I met his worried gaze. "Dr. Awak, these men are not assassins, any more than I am. They're not just hired guns, like you read about in the American Old West. Once they've hired on, you can count on their loyalty. To the end."

"I'm sure of it, Rainey," Leilani put in.

"What you have to understand, Minister," I went on, "is that this little rebellion of yours is pretty well lost, at the moment. Tofa won't tell you this, but your Guard is woefully trained, with little incentive to fight. To change all that and give the government in Apia a chance to defeat Mannheim, we have to have people here who know just what they're doing, people who can fire our troops to fight like tigers. John Boy and Murphy are two such men, Minister."

"You really think that our troops are inferior at the moment?" Awak asked me, his eyes with fear in them.

"I've talked with some officers, including Tupua, who I think is one of your best. Some of your people don't really know how to fire a gun, or have the slightest knowledge of how one works. That all has to be changed, and quickly. Mannheim is ready to move again. And he'll know very soon that I'm training government troops. That will make him act even more quickly."

"Colonel Tupua has followed your instructions and began recruiting young men off the street," Leilani reported to me. 'We're appealing to their new sense of patriotism."

"That's great," I said. "But also tell them their lives are on the line, and the lives of their families. Tell them what will happen if Mannheim should take over here. The executions, the imprisonments, the torturing. Put it on the radio, Minister, on all stations. Drop leaflets into the villages. Take cars with loudspeakers into the streets. Get to the people any way you can, and as fast as you can. You're living on borrowed time right now."

Awak smiled a wan smile. "You sound so . . . frenetic, Rainey. General Tofa says Mannheim won't make any more moves against us for a while, that he'll consolidate his gains in the western part of the island."

"He's already consolidated," I argued. "I've talked to a couple of men who have been in the 'pacified' villages. Mannheim has garrisons in place and well organized. That's apart from the main body of his troops, which are ready to move at any moment. They're apparently better armed than even you imagined, Doctor, and there are more of them. Tupua's reliable sources say they may be as much as several thousand strong."

Awak's face seemed to go a little paler than before. "It seems that I sat here and hoped for peace too long, Rainey. Maybe I sought you out too late."

"I don't think so," I said. "If I did, I wouldn't have taken your commission. But it's important that we lose no more time. And that we know who our enemies are." I said the last deliberately, and both Awak and his daughter studied my face.

"Political opposition is not treason, Rainey," Awak finally said to me. "I've had my differences with both Deputy Minister Mataafa and General Tofa, but neither has given me cause to fear for any unlawful action against me."

"Not yet, anyway," I said.

Leilani laughed lightly. "Come on, Rainey. Let me buy you a lunch at our Indonesian restaurant nearby. That will allay your suspicions about your potential enemies, with some good food in your stomach."

It was apparent that neither Awak nor Leilani was taking what I had said seriously. It was frustrating, but there was little I could do about it at the moment.

I grinned a wry grin. "Okay, Leilani. I'll take you up on that. I'll be in touch with you later about my restructuring of your Apia garrison, Minister."

"I will look forward to our next meeting," Awak assured me.

Leilani and I had a leisurely lunch at a rather nice restaurant only a few blocks from Government House. She was friendly, warm, and sensual. She kept hinting at the fact that we had not been intimate since that first night in Pago Pago. After that meal was finished and we were sipping at aperitifs recommended by Leilani, I finally answered her.

"The turn-on is mutual, baby. But I think we should cool it for a while."

"Whatever for, Rainey?" she asked with those big black eyes.

I shrugged noncommittally. "The kind of work I'm doing and the kind of fun we had the other night don't seem to mix well usually," I told her. "Not when both of the people involved are also involved in the business. I've tried it, believe me."

"I suspect you've tried a little of everything," she said.

"Yeah. I guess I have."

"I would not have expected you to be a cautious man," she commented.

I grinned. "I'm always cautious with women. Once burned, you don't forget easily."

"And you were burned?"

"A long time ago."

"In America?"

"In Paris, after the Asian war. But she was American."

"Did you marry her?"

"Almost."

"Did she say no when you asked her?" Leilani smiled a coy smile.

I was straight-faced. "I had a ring all picked out. We were going to do it at Notre Dame, in a chapel there with a few friends. Then she died on me."

Leilani's face clouded over. "Oh, God. I'm sorry, Rainey."

"It was fast," I said, remembering. "She hadn't told me, but she had this heart valve problem. I got to see her before it was over, but it was all just a blur for me. Then she was gone. Like she was never there, for Christ's sake. Hell, I had seen death in the war. That was different. For me, at least. I went through a bad time."

She watched my face. "I can see that."

"It was crazy, I didn't want that moment in time to slip away from me, even though it tore my guts out. It was like the whole goddamn world should have ended when her life did, and I guess I resented that it just went on, almost without notice. I wanted that moment frozen in time. If it didn't recede into the past, I could hang onto that moment when she was still alive, you know what I mean?"

Leilani nodded gravely. "Yes, of course, Rainey."

"It wasn't long after that that I decided to be a professional," I added. "To just spend the rest of my life fighting other people's wars. I guess in the beginning I wanted to be killed, for somebody to shoot me dead. But then I began trying to survive, after a while. I guess I got good at survival. Maybe too good."

"You can't be too good at that," she said.

I looked over at her. "Maybe you're right," I said. I took a deep breath in. "I haven't talked about that in years. I'm sorry I bored you with it."

"I'm not bored," Leilani said. "Believe me, Rainey."

"I think I ought to get back to the barracks," I told her.

"So soon? You sure you won't reconsider taking some time off with me this afternoon?"

I touched her hand across the table. "Not now, Leilani."

She nodded. "I understand."

I don't know why I went into that song-and-dance with her. All it did was pull me down for the rest of that day. I went back to my headquarters building alone, and found officers already carrying out my orders there, drilling the men at the garrison, getting weapons out for firing practice. I had already ordered new weapons from a couple of sources I knew, and they had been promised to me in a few days. When we got them, we would at least be on a par with Mannheim equipment-wise. But our kids still had to be turned into killers. In a war, it's the soldier with the killer instinct that survives and eventually wins the war.

The garrison headquarters in Apia was a compound of buildings surrounding a large drill area, with palm trees and bougainvillea softening the hard lines of the architecture, which looked a little like Spanish colonial. I had moved out of the B.O.Q. already and had set up my living quarters right in the garrison barracks, on the second floor, just across the compound from my new offices—where I commanded the garrison. The offices themselves were spartan but clean, with white-washed walls and a long oak desk and some furniture to sit on. Bamboo shades striped the windows, and a ceiling fan moved the warm air. Within a half-hour of my arrival back there, I had gathered John Boy, Crazy Jake, and Colonel Tupua to discuss immediate plans.

They sat around my office on chairs and a rattan sofa while I summarized my discussion with Awak for them and then suggested ways to get our war moving.

"We'll be training our people in handling our new weaponry within a few days," I said to them. "I expect our first shipment of guns and ammo by Thursday. From a dealer in Australia. There will be M16 automatic rifles, M16A1's with forty-millimeter M203 grenade launchers, some Colt

CMG-2 light, handheld machineguns, a few fifty-caliber M85C's, and even a few antitank guns to knock out Mannheim's armored personnel carriers, which I hear he has."

Crazy Jake looked different from that night in Pago Pago. He was shaved now, wore a green uniform like mine and the others, and looked almost human. He was slumped onto a leather chair in one corner of the office. "I got the rocket mortars coming by Saturday," he reported to me. "That bastard that used to sell hard drugs to kids in Central American, remember? Name of Bernini. He'd also promised us three rocket cannons, Russians."

John Boy, looking like somebody fresh out of West Point, grinned that schoolboy grin. "With that kind of stuff we can lick the goddamn Marines."

I glanced over at him where he sat looking spit-and-polish on the rattan sofa. "If we had people who could use them," I said. "We've got a lot of work ahead of us, and damned little time to do it."

Tupua sat near my desk on a rather elegant straight chair that looked out of place in Samoa. It was in the English Tudor style, and looked too fragile for Tupua to sit on. Tupua had agreed to my command of the combat battalion, to act as my second in command despite his equal and permanent rank. When the fighting started, I expected each of the four of us to lead a company of assault forces against Mannheim, with Jake and John Boy sharing equal command with Tupua.

"You will be pleasantly surprised at the eagerness of our troops to learn, I think," Tupua offered. He looked rather squat and broad next to Crazy Jake and John Boy. He had met them on the previous evening, and they all had seemed to like each other. Jake had grown an immediate respect for Tupua when he learned that Tupua had once shot it out with a soldier in a bar, taken three bullets in the body, and survived. His opponent had gone straight to the morgue. "Our people are not natural warriors, but when their homeland is threatened, they always respond."

"I'm sure they will, Colonel," I said. "The question is whether Mannheim will give us much time for that response. The rumor is that he's planning another move toward Apia soon, to take more of the countryside under his control."

"We have small garrisons in villages in his path," Tupua said.

"I know. Pull them out immediately," I told him.

He frowned. "And give Mannheim a free hand to advance on us?"

"Those people of ours out there are nothing more than farmers carrying guns," I reminded him. "He'll massacre them as he's already massacred others of your troops. Bring them back in here to Apia, Colonel, before they give up their lives foolishly. They will join our combat battalion here, and get training and modern weaponry. Then we'll use them against Mannheim effectively."

"And in the meantime?" Tupua said.

"In the meantime Mannheim will advance without resistance," I said. "He'll be lulled into a false sense of security because it's all so easy. Then, hopefully, in a couple of weeks we'll go meet him on the battlefield. If we're lucky, he won't be expecting what we'll have ready for him."

"We'll make the sonofabitch wish he'd stayed in Germany," John Boy said in a hard voice.

Jake looked at John Boy and then at me, and grinned. Jake liked to hear words like that come out of the mouth of a fuzz-faced kid. Jake had a sense of humor when he was sober, and that was funny to him. I returned the grin.

"I got a message from him," Jake said. "Through an informant. Mannheim didn't like my little defection. Said he'll settle with me before this is over."

Tupua turned to him. "Did you send a reply?"

Jake took out a cheap cigar and chewed on it. "Yeah. I said that by the time this was over, I'll pull his goddamn liver out and boil it in a stew."

Tupua stared hard at Crazy Jake, then laughed uncertainly. "Yes. Yes, of course, Captain Murphy."

John Boy laughed, too. But it was because he knew that Jake was not joking. In Namibia once, an African chief had offered Jake a portion of heart cut from an enemy soldier earlier that day, telling Jake the soldier had been very brave, and that Jake would add that bravery to his own by eating of that vital organ. Jake had surprised and disgusted some other mercs by actually eating some of the heart. It was after that that they began calling him "Crazy" Jake.

"Mannheim sounds like a sore loser," I said. "Which makes him a dangerous opponent. Let's not ever forget that." I looked over at John Boy. "You said you had a lead for us on Tofa. Have you developed it yet?"

John Boy nodded. "I found an informant who knew this retired colonel. Name of Matautu."

"I know him," Tupua said. "But he was really before my time. A loyal officer in the police who was given a rank in the new Civil Guard just before his retirement from service. An honorable man, I believe."

"I checked him out," John Boy said. "He's reliable, and he has no personal axe to grind against Tofa."

"So what's all this leading up to, kid?" Crazy Joe asked a little impatiently.

John Boy turned to him. "I think you ought to hear what he has to say from his own mouth."

"Okay," I said. "When can we talk to him?"

John Boy grinned. "He's outside now, in the corridor. Waiting to talk to you."

I made a face. "Why the hell didn't you say so, John Boy? Go get him, will you?"

John Boy left grinning, and in a moment returned with a rather frail, gray-haired man wearing expense slacks and shirt and Italian shoes. He nodded to all of us, and then addressed Tupua. "It is a pleasure to meet with you again, Colonel Tupua." In a weak, quiet voice.

Tupua and I had risen from our chairs. "The pleasure is mutual, Colonel," Tupua told him. "This is Colonel Rainey, our new Commander here at the garrison. Also Captains Murphy and Reese." The kid's new name.

After the introductions Matautu sat on the sofa beside John Boy. John Boy turned to him. "Tell them what you told me earlier, Colonel," he said.

Matautu nodded, and looked across the office to

me. "I have a youngish nephew who has hired on with Mannheim, Colonel Rainey," he began in his soft voice. "He was an officer in the police here, and was recruited by Mannheim's people. Most of the family has disowned him since. Through his auspices, someone also came to me to get me to join up with the rebels. I angrily declined. Mannheim is arming a mob of criminals, Colonel. And he wants them to take over our beautiful islands."

"That much I know," I said to him.

"Well, recently this nephew sneaked back into Apia and spoke with another young relative to recruit him. He was unsuccessful, but in the conversation, in his eagerness to persuade this other young man, he let something slip that is top secret."

"About General Tofa?" I said.

"Yes, about Tofa. He told this other young man that General Tofa has met with Mannheim. It seems they had a long talk, Colonel. And they made a deal."

"What kind of a deal?" I said.

"When Mannheim reached Apia with almost no opposition from the Civil Guard, Tofa will surrender the Civil Guard and police to Mannheim without a fight, and declare Mannheim the new Prime Minister by *de facto* right."

"And Tofa will get what?" I asked.

"Tofa will be Mannheim's Deputy Minister and head of all the military forces in the islands," Matautu said. "They will rule Samoa with an iron hand."

"I'll be damned," John Boy said in a whisper. "That part's news."

"That sonofabitch promised me chief of police,"

Crazy Jake grumbled. "Tofa would have stood me up against a wall, by God."

Tupua was still reacting. He rose from his chair. "Are you sure about this?" he said in a hushed voice.

Matautu nodded. "Very sure."

"Why didn't you come to us before?" Tupua accused him.

Matautu shrugged. "I don't know. I'm retired, Colonel. I didn't want to get involved in all of this again. When these people came to me, I felt obligated to come forward."

"You did the right thing, Colonel," I told him.

"This is an outrage!" Tupua was saying now, sputtering over his new knowledge about Tofa. "I knew that Tofa was a self-serving bastard, but this is unconscionable!"

"I never liked the man" Matautu said. "But I assure you that had nothing to do with my coming here, gentlemen."

"That bastard Mannheim," Crazy Jake was still saying under his breath.

John Boy looked over at me. "Pretty big stuff, huh, Rainey?"

I nodded to him. "Pretty big stuff. But not unexpected by me, by God. Colonel Matautu, I can't tell you how grateful we are that you came to us with this. If there's anything we can do to repay you just let us know."

"I don't want payment," Matautu said. "Just do what has to be done, Colonel Rainey. So we may enjoy these islands as we have for thousands of years."

"We're working on that," I siad. I rose. "Thanks

again, Colonel. If you hear anything more, we'd appreciate your sharing it with us."

He promised he would, and then he was gone. I swore them all to secrecy about Tofa, then I called Dr. Awak and asked for an appointment with him in which Mataafa and Tofa would be present. Awak agreed. We would all meet the following evening at Tofa's office in Government House, because Awak intended to see Tofa there anyway. When those arrangements had been made, I dismissed Tupua and Crazy Jake and had a short private conference with John Boy. He moved over to a chair beside my oak desk, where I sat tapping a pencil on a note pad thoughtfully.

"God knows how many spies we have here in Apia, in the government and the Guard, with Tofa on their side," I said. "We'll have to seek them out, John Boy. And we ought to have somebody in with Mannheim too. To find out what he's plannng for the next few weeks. Do you know any subordinate officers well enough yet to recommend somebody for such a dangerous assignment?"

John Boy grinned that disarming grin. "Let me go, Rainey."

"What? Are you crazy? I need you here!"

"I'll return here in time to take over a battle company," he argued with me. "What you need right now is somebody you can trust on the other side. Somebody with experience at this sort of thing. I did this in Nicaragua, Rainey. Undercover work. I got good at it. I'll to to Mannheim and ask for the job that Jake turned down. Tell him Jake was nuts for turning his back on that high pay, and I'm happy to make it instead of him. Give him some bullshit. Hell, I can handle it. He'll want to believe me."

"Mueller and Rabbit Burroughs are no dummies, John Boy," I reminded him. "They know you better than Mannheim, remember. And Rabbit will resent your presence there. Be loooking for ways to put you down. He'll be suspicious from the outset. Can you handle all of that?"

"Rabbit is shit under my feet," John Boy said sourly. "I can make that jerk believe anything I want him to. Don't sweat it, Rainey. Let me go, and within a week I'll be back here with all of Mannheim's strategies laid out in front of you."

He was convincing. He was right about one thing too. I needed somebody for cloak-and-dagger at the moment more than I needed a company commander.

I thought a moment, then grinned. "You better take off that West Point outfit before you go over. Mannheim will have to stretch his imagination to see you as a rebel in that."

"Then I can go?" John Boy said excitedly.

"You can go."

"When?"

"How about tonight?" I suggested.

His face lighted up. "Right on!" he grinned.

John Boy disappeared that night, on his way to the battle front where Mannheim had pacified some villages. He was to stay only one week and then report back. I crossed my fingers for him, and hoped.

The next morning Matautu showed up again unexpectedly, without an invitation this time, and brought a very scared relative who corroborated his story about Tofa's defection to Mannheim. I didn't need any more proof than that. I got on the phone to Awak and told him I needed the emergency meeting with him, Tofa, and Mataafa as soon as he could firm it up.

"The General is difficult to get to see nowadays," Awak told me on the phone. "He doesn't answer his telephone. It is not set yet."

I wondered about a setup in which a general is out to a prime minister, but I kept my silence. "Send him a personal messenger," I told Awak. "This is important to you, Minister."

A short silence. "All right. I will try again for a meeting with both men for this evening."

I didn't hint to Awak what I had learned about Tofa. I wanted to drop it as a bombshell at the meeting later. I wanted to be sure that Tofa heard it from me for the first time, and had no time to react to it in advance.

We met at Tofa's office in the big old colonial building at eight that evening. I took Crazy Jake, both of us dressed in the same uniform as Tofa, both armed. Jake carried his Webley revolver on his hip, and I had purchased a Browning Mark I 9mm automatic from a local store. It was a hefty weapon built a lot like the Colt .45, but not with the Colt's elephant-gun power.

Awak brought Leilani again to the meeting, and I was beginning to realize how much he leaned on his beautiful daughter. I was sorry to see her there, considering what was going down. They were there ahead of us, waiting for Tofa and Mataafa to show. There was an armed guard outside the office, and one placed inside. They both carried M-1 rifles at their sides. Awak seemed disturbed by their presence, but I had expected it. Leilani smiled warmly when she saw me, and I knew she was still on the make for me. Awak advised me that Mataafa and Tofa would both be there presently.

Mataafa arrived in a couple of minutes, looking very rich in a white tropical worsted suit and Gucci shoes. If ever a man looked the part of a crook, it was Mataafa.

"I understand you're the instigator of this late rendezvous, Colonel Rainey," he said in his oily voice to me. "I hope it doesn't take long. I have an appointment with a very handsome lady later." He grinned a clever grin.

I gave Awak a look. "It shouldn't take long, Minister. After the general gets here."

Mataafa looked me over, and then glanced at Crazy Jake. "Your appearance frankly surprises me, Colonel. You look like a . . . real soldier suddenly."

"Uniforms don't make soldiers, Mataafa," I said.

"I'll agree with that," Dr. Awak put in. He looked very sick to me, and like he was impatient for this to be over with. I saw how a government could go to hell under these circumstances.

"But the uniform does give a man a certain . . . bearing, don't you think?" Leilani said, giving me a hungry look.

"Well, in my opinion," Mataafa said, "a military look—"

But at that moment he was interrupted by General Tofa's appearance. Tofa strode into the room briskly, and stopped just inside the open doorway. He looked around. He looked very blocky and tough, standing there in his gold braid and medals. He removed a peaked cap and spoke to Awak. "Good evening, Minister. Mataafa. He glanced at me and Jake, and did not speak. He walked over to a long teak desk across a carpeted floor, and turned to Leilani. "And the beautiful lady. What an illustrious gathering."

"We are here at Colonel Rainey's request, General," Awak told him.

Tofa gave me a quick blistering look. "Ah. Already the general is summoned by the upstart colonel who is not a colonel."

"Oh God," Leilani muttered.

"This is not a summons in any way," Awak said apologetically. He was standing beside Tofa's desk, and Tofa stood behind it, looking very much in charge of the situation and the islands. If I hadn't known better, I would have thought it was Tofa who was running the government, not Awak. "Colonel Rainey merely wishes to discuss a military matter that has arisen with some urgency. Isn't that true, Colonel?"

I eyed Awak for a moment, then turned to Tofa. "This is going to be a very private matter we'll be discussing. I'd like to do it without the presence of military guards."

Tofa scowled at me arrogantly. "Now you tell me whom I should have on duty at my headquarters, Rainey? What an impertinent bastard you are! My two personal guards stay. One inside this office!"

Crazy Jake gave me a quick look, and I acknowledged it. "Okay, General. If that's the way you want it. May I at least close the door for privacy?"

"Go ahead," Tofa said grimly.

I closed the door on the outside guard, and now we had only one inside to hear what was going down. He stood at ease near the doorway, the M-1's butt on the carpeted floor. Tofa himself wore a Brazilian revolver on his hip, a Civil Guard issue.

I turned back to him. Crazy Jake stood on the opposite side of the room from the armed guard, with his feet slightly apart. He looked even tougher than Tofa, standing there with his scarred face and hard look. Leilani had helped Awak onto a leather chair beside Tofa's desk, and now she went and sat herself on a straight chair on the same wall as Jake. Jake looked her over hungrily and she did not notice.

"All right, Rainey," Tofa said in his metallic voice. "You have the whole damned government here tonight. What the hell is so important that you take us all away from important matters outside office hours?"

He was going to be as difficult as ever. That made it better for me. It made the whole thing more satisfying.

"I've already conceded several organizational charges that give you unprecedented power at your rank," Tofa went on. "What do you want now, Rainey? My job?"

I walked over to the desk, and stood beside it, on the other side from where Awak was sitting. "Why haven't you moved against Mannheim, Tofa?"

He grew a deep scowl on his broad, thick face. "What?"

"Why haven't you organized at attack force like

we're doing now? Why have you made no move against Mannhiem with real force? Why have you allowed his buildup to go so far without real opposition?"

The scowl deepened to show his sudden rage. "You damned outsider! How dare you challenge my military decisions here in my own islands! I don't have to explain anything to you, you American bum!" He turned hostily to Awak. "Is this what we've come to, Fiame? Did you set this meeting up to allow this imposter soldier to insult me and my reputation here among my people? Do you know what reaction the *matai* would have to this kind of abuse of your power?"

Awak held up a hand. "I had no idea what Colonel Rainey intended here, General. But let us allow him to have his say."

"I agree with the general," Mataafa put in mildly. "We told you there would be trouble, letting a foreigner, a stranger, come into our midst and dictate policy to us. It is the result of your sickness, Minister. I warned you about it."

"My illness has nothing to do with this!" Awak said harshly. He knew that Mataafa was just waiting to take over governmental responsibility, hoping for Awak to show incapacity.

"My father is perfectly capable of running the government of Western Samoa," Leilani said coldly to Mataafa. "And his decision to commission Rainey in the Guard was a wise one, and badly needed."

Tofa turned to Leilani belligerently, then back to Awak. "Do we need this woman's presence in every meeting of state?" he said in a low growl. "Can we accomplish nothing without her advice and counsel?"

Awak regarded Tofa bleakly. "My daughter's help in the ministry has been invaluable, General. She is a loyal Somoan wanting only to make whatever contribution she can to keeping this government together."

"You don't have to concern yourself with me at all, General," Leilani said. "I wield no power here, hold no authority. But it is still legal in Samoa to express an opinion. To my father or anybody else I so wish."

I sat on the edge of Tofa's desk and lit a Cuban cigar. He gave me a hard look as I puffed it into life and then dropped a match into a cut-glass ashtray on his immaculate desk.

"I think we're getting away from things here," I said. "The general hasn't answered my questions."

"And I don't intend to, you sonofabitch!" Tofa spat at me. "It is only because of respect for the minister here that I don't have you arrested by my personal guard!"

Crazy Jake laughed softly in his throat, and Tofa and the others turned quizzically to him.

I continued, addressing myself to Awak now. "I had a talk with one of your retired colonels," I told him. "Your General Tofa here has sold you out. Made a deal with Mannheim."

Awak's jaw fell slightly open. Leilani turned slowly to stare at Tofa, and so did Mataafa. I saw the guard at the door grasp his rifle more tightly.

Tofa himself registered several emotions on his hard face before he showed the anger again. There was surprise, shock, fear, and black resolve there, in turn. He waited a very long moment before he spoke, to compose himself. Then his reply came in a grating voice.

"What the hell are you talking about?" he whispered.

The office had fallen deadly silent. I took the cigar from my mouth and studied its glowing end. "Five weeks ago, on a Friday night. You and Mannheim met at a village called Apolima. You had a long private meeting there, in which you discussed the future of Samoa. You agreed to let Mannheim come on to Apia, where you would surrender your entire Civil Guard to his rebel forces. In return for a high post in his new government."

Leilani rose from her chair. "I'll be damned!" she said.

Awak also rose, staring hard at Tofa. Mataafa arched his dark brows, but said nothing.

"You had also met with him on a previous occasion, when he made the offer to you," I added. "You've sold out, Tofa. You plan to help run a dictatorship here in the islands worse than anything since Adolf Hitler."

Tofa was under control again. He fumed and sputtered, turning to Awak. "Do you believe this criminal who hires his gun to any group who pays him? Do you really think there is any truth in this?"

"The colonel who gave me the information is Matautu," I said to Awak.

Awak swore under his breath. "Matautu's word is unimpeachable," he said quietly to Tofa.

Tofa acted outraged. "This is incredible!" he said. "This is a pack of lies! I demand that this man and

Matautu be arrested and interrogated by my officers! We will soon squeeze the truth out of them!"

Awak hesitated, then spoke. "You will arrest no one, General. I believe what Rainey has told us."

Tofa turned to Awak arrogantly. "Do you think you are really in charge here? I don't have to explain my relations with Mannheim to you or anybody else! As always, you will sit back and allow others to act for you, Minister! Don't concern yourself, things are being taken care of just as they should be!"

"How dare you!" Leilani sputtered.

I took a deep breath in. "Tofa," I said, catching his attention.

He turned dark-eyed to me.

"This isn't just between you and the minister now," I said. "It's between you and me."

"You and me!" he fumed. "You are a bug under my foot, Rainey! You're through here! Don't you understand that?"

"No, it's you that's through," I said. "I'm giving you a choice, Tofa. If you agree to get on a plane tonight, under my guard, and fly away from here forever, I'll let this all pass. Otherwise, I can't."

"Fly out of . . . You'll let it pass!" he sputtered, his broad face a mask of rage. "Well, let me tell you what is what, Rainey! I can take over this weakling's government by merely raising a hand! I don't even need Mannheim! If I say so, none of you in this room will leave this building tonight!"

"I said nothing against you, General," Mataafa reminded him nervously.

I sighed. I had figured this was the way it would be.

"In a matter of hours," Tofa was saying loudly, "I will—"

I drew the Browning pistol from its holster at my hip, aimed it at Tofa's head, and squeezed the trigger. There was a deafening explosion in the room, and the hot slug from the automatic hit Tofa in the right cheek. His head whiplashed and a fragment of his skull blew away at the back as he threw his arms outward, a look of abject surprise on his heavy features, and slammed against the wall behind the desk.

A moment later he slid to the floor, and left a long stain on the paneled wall. He had been dead when he crashed into the wall.

Leilani, Awak, and Mataafa stood in stunned silence, and the guard at the door finally reacted. He lifted the M-1 to kill me, but Crazy Jake had already drawn his Webley. Jake put one shot into the guard, at chest level, and the guard banged against the closed door, then stumbled forward and hit the floor on his face, shot through the heart.

In the next instant, the door crashed open and the second guard stood there, looking wild-eyed. He glimpsed Tofa on the floor, and raised the rifle toward me. I fired first, and lifted him off his booted feet. He went running backwards into the outer office and crashed across a desk and chair there, taking the chair down with him. The rifle fired off a round into the ceiling, and he was lifeless on the floor.

I holstered the Browning. Awak was cowering in a corner now, fear marring his thin features. Mataafa was in a crouch, behind the desk, looking like he was going to be sick. Leilani just stood there, breathing shallowly, watching me closely with those big eyes.

Awak and Mataafa stood upright again, and Awak leaned against the corner of the long desk. "My God!" he said weakly. He was trembling slightly.

Mataafa was staring at the bloody head of Tofa, whose eyes still stared in open surprise at his sudden demise. Jake stood near me, casually examining the magazine of the Webley, looking as if nothing had happened.

"I'm sorry, Minister," I said to Awak. "But it was absolutely necessary. Tofa intended to do that to you. Tonight. Or next week. He was past negotiation."

"I . . . understand," Awak said.

"You did . . . what you had to do," Leilani said breathlessly to me. She had been excited by the gunfire and death, but not afraid. I was impressed.

I turned to Jake. "Call Colonel Tupua. Have him come over here immediately and take command of the guard," I said.

"Right, Rainey," Jake said. He disappeared from the room.

I turned back to the others. "Mataafa, I want your resignation in Dr. Awak's office tomorrow morning."

Mataafa stared hard at me. "What?"

"You're no damned good, Mataafa," I said. "You have no place in what we're doing here."

Awak looked at me for a long moment, then over to Mataafa. "Rainey is right, Tupuola. I knew you had no business in government, from the moment I was elected. Let the *matai* scream. We can't tolerate self-serving boors in my cabinet, not now."

Mataafa didn't make the same fight as Tofa. He was scared of Jake and me now. "All right," he finally said. "You'll have it in writing early tomorrow morning, Minister. But there are going to be many families displeased by this action."

"Then let them go join with Mannheim!" Awak said firmly.

Mataafa left the room then, not making further comments to us. I turned to Awak. "We'll clean up this mess, Minister. You and Leilani should go home and get some rest. Tomorrow, you can announce that Tofa was a traitor who was killed in resisting arrest by loyal troops."

Awak nodded. "I'm not sure I approve of your methods, Colonel. But I want to thank you for ridding us of a traitor in our midst."

"We're not in a situation where we can practice niceties of the law," I said. "I fight my enemies on their level, Minister. I found out that if I don't, they're liable to win. And I hate losing. I'll fight Mannheim the same way. And with a little luck, I'll help you save Samoa; and your own lives."

"It's an end devoutly to be wished," Awak said gravely.

FIVE

The people of Apia took the killing of Tofa without any expression of emotion whatever. I think they were waiting to see what kind of people me and my men were, and what kind of alternate leadership we were going to offer. Within a week, against my objections, Awak made me general of the entire Civil Guard, and I incorporated the police into the Guard for the time being. I established a military government in Samoa, with strict martial law in effect, curfews and the whole works. I promoted Crazy Jake Murphy to colonel, and planned to do the same with John Boy when he returned from Mannheim's camp.

That was giving me some worry, John Boy's absence. His week was up and he wasn't back, and I had had no word from him. I got a bad feeling inside me about it. I had sent him into a goddamn lion's den and I felt responsible, even though he had twisted my arm to go.

In that week after Tofa's death, we received a lot

of weapony. We got thousands of M-16 automatic rifles, several hundred M-16A1 rifles with grenade launchers, light and heavy machineguns, mortars, recoilless rifles, antitank missiles. The cannons never came, but we also got hold of a few dozen trucks and Jeeps for transportation of personnel and equipment. Tofa had been in charge of the whole damned show, and had left the Guard with its pants down. We didn't even have necessary equipment for bivouac at field camps. It had had to get it all, but most of it was now there. We were beginning to look like an army.

The troops were still green, but they were learning every day. With John Boy gone, though, it fell primarily on me and Jake to get the men trained for what was to come. War. Most of them had never been fired at in battle. We recruited new people too, and our force grew. Things were shaping up. Very soon our assault battalion would be equal to Mannheim's rebel force, at least in terms of numbers. Whether it could fight as well remained to be seen.

It was almost two weeks since John Boy had departed for Mannheim's HQ when Crazy Jake and Colonel Tupua came into my garrison HQ office one afternoon, fresh in from a troop bivouac. Jake looked like he had just come out of a muddy foxhole, in his soiled fatigues. He was the kind who always got right down in the dirt with the troops, and I liked that about him. The scar on his cheek was pink from exertion, and he still carried an M-16 rifle at his side. He slumped onto a sofa I had had put in the room, with two bandoliers still slung across his chest. Tupua appeared neater in his fatigues, but seemed very weary. He slumped beside Jake.

"Well, they're shaping up," Jake told me tiredly. Then he added sourly, "In about five years, they'll look like U.S. Marines."

I grinned from behind my paper-piled desk, and Tupua grinned too. "Jake has done a miracle with his people," he admitted. "His knowledge of firearms is amazing."

"Shit," Jake said in a growl. "It's all just shooting, Tupua."

But Tupua was right. Jake's commander in Lebanon said Jake could take an AK-47 apart and put it back together inside a zipped body bag, and I'd guess he was right.

"I don't think they'll ever learn to use the grenade-launchers the way they should be used," Tupua fretted. "And we're having a lot of trouble teaching them range-finding with the rocket mortars, especially on the night patrol we took them on. But we must remember that General Mannheim has the same problems with his untrained people."

"*General* Mannheim?" I said.

"That is the rank he has taken to himself," Tupua told me. "I think his creating rank in his army of rabble was a move in the right direction for him, and I respect him for it. I refer to him by his chosen rank because it reminds me that he is in fact the military leader of a sizable and formidable force."

I thought about that a minute, and decided Tupua was right. "Okay," I said. "General Mannheim it is. Do you think we're ready to move out into the field with these people?"

Tupua shrugged. "I suppose we could always be reluctant to move, no matter how much training was given. I think they are ready to fight, General Rainey."

I had never been given such a lofty rank in all my years of fighting other people's wars, and it made me uncomfortable every time I heard someone call me by my rank. "That's a lot more important than how much they know about field equipment," I said. "Have you gotten any information back yet about possible co-conspirators with Tofa?"

Crazy Jake set his rifle down heavily. "I just got briefed on the situation by the captain we put in charge. There are two colonels and a major who admit they were in with Tofa."

"They admitted it?" I said.

Jake grinned darkly. "Under questioning, of course."

I grunted. I had to keep Jake on a short leash.

"Colonel Murphy did not use methods that were offensive to me and other Samoan officers," Tupua said. "These men are vermin among us and are not entitled to kid-glove treatment, General."

"What do you want us to do with them?" Jake asked me.

I studied my desk top, staring at all the paper work there. It was time to get out into the field, before all the paper buried me. "Are you sure of their guilt?" I said.

"We are very sure, General," Tupua answered for Jake.

I sighed heavily. "Then I think we have no choice. Get a firing squad ready. And I want the entire HQ garrison to witness the executions."

"Yes, General," Tupua said.

"We have to take a stand against treason," I said. "I want to be damned sure of the loyalty of the people we end up with out there."

"Likewise," Crazy Jake agreed.

Tupua started to add something to Jake's comment, but there was a knock on my office door. I got up and walked over to it. There was no carpeting in my office, no fancy paintings or potted plants. It was spartan because I had stripped all that kind of stuff out of there when I took over the room. There was a Samoan flag in a corner, a big gun rack on one wall—with an example of each type of small arms we were now using in the rack, and a rocket mortar sitting in the middle of the room not far from my desk. I wanted anybody that walked in to be reminded we were are war. I opened the door, and a sentry stood there with a uniformed courier beside him.

"General, this man says he has a message for you. From the camp of the enemy."

I glanced at the small, thin courier. "This is from John Boy?"

"Yes, sir. I waited at the place chosen, and he came."

Jake got up from the sofa and came over beside me. I took a folded paper from the sentry, and opened it. There was a message in John Boy's handwriting. I grinned and looked at Jake, and he returned the grin.

"Thanks, soldier. Return to the rendezvous point and take up your vigil there."

"Yes, sir."

I closed the door and returned to my desk, and

seated myself there. I studied the note from John Boy. It was a relief just to know he was alive.

"What does he have to say, General?" Tupua asked.

"It's in Swahili," I said. "We both know the language and figured it would be a good enough code here in Samoa. It says that Mannheim has taken two more villages and has immediate plans to move his army toward Apia."

"Damn!" Jake said excitedly. He was over-ripe for the fighting we all knew was coming.

"It seems Mannheim's war is upon us," Tupua said.

"Yes," I agreed. "John Boy also says that Mannheim has Russian weapons by the carload—AK-47's, Tokarev pistols, machineguns—and a lot of Latin American stuff. He says we're going to have our hands full."

"I never doubted it," Tupua said.

I sat back on my high-back chair and let the note drop onto the other papers on my desk. I wasn't quite ready myself. I wanted a lot more hours of training for my people, especially in the use of the bigger, heavier weapons. But there was no time for training now. There was only time for fighting. Mannheim had taken the one away from us and handed us the other.

"Okay," I said slowly. "We've got ourselves a war. Jake, Tupua. Pass the word down. We'll start moving out of here tomorrow. The whole damned battalion. With the nearby village garrisons, we ought to have several thousand people. We'll move heavy-equipment companies out first. John Boy says he'll be back here within a couple of days, and he'll be in charge of them in the field. Jake, you get your special assault units ready to march. Tupua, you and I will organize the rifle companies for moving out. It will all begin tomorrow at five a.m. We'll march to the Tutuila Plantation in the central highlands. They ought to meet Mannheim about halfway. We'll set up our battalion command post there for the moment, and take the war up from there."

"I'm by God ready!" Jake said in a low voice.

"We'd better be," I said. "We'd better damned well be."

The next morning we were up and out before dawn with the lead companies of the battalion. I decided to leave with the heavy guns, and rode out in the dark in an unmarked jeep.

The island of Upolu is a kind of small one as islands go, and it did not take our company long to make a journey to the highlands area of Tutuila. At first we drove along a road that was surrounded by marshy swampland and bogs, with jungle-type foliage, where I knew there were slithery things and bugs as dangerous as Mannheim. But then in the sunlight we emerged onto high ground, where there were rocky, open meadows and an occasional copra or coffee plantation. We passed the big Tutuila Plantation on its edge, and I ordered the small army to halt and encamp on a wide sunny meadow, just a few miles beyond the plantation.

A tent camp was set up there, and big trucks hauled weapons and equipment in and dumped them there. Mortars and antitank guns were unloaded, and recoilless rifles. By late morning other companies had rolled in and the tent camp grew big. Swarms of riflemen disembarked from trucks and organized into units. Ammo trucks arrived, and a hospital van and several mess tents were set up.

I didn't want my army to get too comfortable there, though. I figured on taking the war to Mannheim, so these people would not hole up and dig in. That wasn't the way I fought. By late afternoon I was set up in my HQ tent, with tables, cots, the works. Orderlies milled about reporting on the state of our new encampment. Bugles blared in the crisp air. Banners fluttered in a mild breeze. I was beginning to like the look of things. Of course, the tale would be told when my people started getting shot at. So far it was just show and tell. Later the blood would flow.

I don't know why, but I began thinking of Leilani when we got bivouacked out there. She had seemed impressed by my shooting of Tofa, and excited by the incident, and for some reason that made her even more appealing to me than she already was. Also, I felt a little lonely out there in battalion HQ. So, on the evening of our second day there, when Leilani appeared unexpectedly in camp with a driver and two uniformed bodyguards, I was glad to see her.

"I'll be damned," I said when she got out of the jeep in front of my tent.

"Hi, Rainey," she smiled at me. "I have an excuse for coming, don't be angry with me. I brought you a case of brandy, compliments of my father. He says you may need it before this is over." She gestured toward the guards who were carrying the case of liquor to my tent.

"Very thoughtful of him," I said. "In more ways than one."

Leilani looked great. She wore a fatigue uniform, but it didn't hide many of her curves. Her hair was down and long, and blowing in a light breeze. She made my groin tingle, just looking at her.

I asked her inside the tent, dismissed an orderly in there, and closed the tent flap. It was getting dark outside, and there would soon be a lights-out bugle. I poured us a tin cup of the brandy each, and we sipped it sitting on straight chairs facing each other.

"I dismissed my driver," she finally said. "For the night."

"Oh?'"

"I hoped to find someone here who would share quarters with me until tomorrow morning," she said with a coy smile.

"Hmmph," I said. "I wonder who that might be."

She widened the smile. "This tent seems large enough to share," she suggested.

I looked around. "I might be able to fit you in somewhere here," I said. "Maybe bring another cot in."

She gave me a look and got up and came over and sat down on my lap, and put her arm over my shoulder. She lightly kissed me on my cheek. "You turn me on, Rainey. When you shot that bastard Tofa, I wanted you to rape me right there. In front of everybody, with their eyes wide in shock."

I squinted down on her. "No shit."

"I mean it. You make me breathless with your masculine aggressiveness. Can't you see that?" She kissed my ear, and my neck. I swigged the rest of my brandy.

"I see you got yourself worked up," I said. "That's hard for a man to turn away from, Leilani. The knowledge that a girl has the hots for him. You knew that when you came, didn't you?"

She nodded, and set her brandy down on the floor. "Do you have the hots for me, Rainey?"

I hesitated. "I guess I do," I said.

She unbuttoned her tunic and took it off, and I stared at her in her skimpy bra. God, she was put together. "It can be even better than that first night, Rainey. I can do things for you that we didn't have time for then." She opened her mouth slightly, and ran her tongue over her lips. Her hand dropped down to my waist and unfastened my belt buckle, and her soft behind moved on my legs. I reached and grabbed a handful of soft flesh and my mouth went dry. She was a very sexy woman.

"Kiss me, Rainey," she whispered.

I did, and her tongue explored my mouth. My hands were mauling her now almost without my thinking about it. We were both breathless when the bugle sounded not far away.

"That's lights out," I said.

"How convenient," she said sensually.

She got off me and went and turned an oil lamp down, and the tent went dark. I could just barely see her now, in the light from a mosquito-netting window. I went to the tent flap and spoke to a sentry outside.

"I don't want to be disturbed until reveille," I said.

"Yes, sir," came the knowing reply.

I lowered the flap again and turned back to Leilani. She had stripped down to panties, and she was all curves. She came over to me and undressed me, kissing me all the time. I loved it. I needed the relaxation. In a few minutes we were on my cot together, and it was like before, only a lot better, like Leilani had promised. She took her time in getting me heated up, and she was very good at what she did. When we finally made it, I was past ready. There was a hot union and a violent copulation and a lot of love cries coming from Leilani's arched throat. The sentry outside must have gotten quite a show from the noise we made. When it was finished I couldn't bring myself to separate us. It all felt too warm, too tingly, too good.

A little later we fell asleep, and then when we woke we made it again, and then more sleep. It was about three in the a.m. when I woke up again, this time with the sentry calling me.

I sat up on the cot beside Leilani. She was sleeping nude beside me, and it was a sight to behold. All curved flesh and warm breathing. I wondered about her reaction to the killing of Tofa, realizing there was more to her than appeared on the surface. I pulled on a pair of O.D. shorts, stumbled to the front of the tent, and pulled the flap open.

The sentry stood there, his face grave. "I'm sorry, General. I know you didn't want to be disturbed, but—"

"What the hell is it, Sergeant?" I growled. "Do you know what time it is?"

"Yes, sir. But I thought you'd want to know."

"Yes?" I said impatiently.

He turned and pointed, and I saw the other soldiers for the first time. They had carried a thing up to the tent and put it on the ground on a piece of plastic. I squinted down at it, and saw there was a body there.

"What the hell is this?" I said.

"They found this dead man outside a nearby village, after an informant came to one of our outpost sentries," he said. "We think it must be the other American."

My heart jumped in my chest. I walked over to the figure on the ground, as I heard Leilani come out of the tent behind me. I glanced back at her. She had thrown a robe around her nakedness, and stood staring at the dead body before me. She recognized the figure immediately, and I heard a small gasp issue from her throat.

I looked down, and she was right. It was John Boy, no doubt about it. I have never seen a more bloody corpse. His eyes had been probed out and there were only bloody sockets left. His tongue had also been cut out, and his ears sliced off. Then they had disemboweled him. On his bared chest somebody had carved a letter *R*. For Rabbit Burroughs. It was his signature, so to speak.

"You bastards," I said in a low, hollow voice. "You bloody, soulless bastards!"

SIX

It took me a couple of days to get over John Boy's killing.

I had recruited him, I had sent him into an enemy camp I knew was dangerous for him in the extreme.

Now he was dead.

Murdered in a brutal, savage way.

I had known that Rabbit was a goddamn snake, but I had never seen one professional do something like that to another. There was an unwritten code among mercs, that we should behave ourselves in a civilized way toward each other.

Rabbit had violated that code.

In the ugliest way possible.

Rabbit had vowed to kill me in this coming confrontation. Now I vowed the same about him. I wanted that sonofabitch dead. I wanted him in hell with his back broke.

Leilani had returned to Apia that next morning after our reunion in bed, and had taken the news with her about John Boy's death, so that everybody in the capital knew, as well as our troops. It was demoralizing, and that was why it had been done in that vicious way. Mannheim had allowed Rabbit to practice his butchery so that our people would be scared to death of what would happen to them if they chose the wrong side in this war.

He had made his point.

When Crazy Jake saw the corpse of John Boy, the next morning, he promised me Rabbit's head on a pole. I lied to him, and told him Rabbit had no more value to me than any other soldier under Mannheim. I couldn't afford to encourage personal vedettas. They could get you killed needlessly.

"We can't just ignore this, Rainey," he told me sitting in my tend that morning, after we had buried John Boy. "Send me to one of the villages where Mannheim keeps small garrisons. I'll capture some of his people, and we'll send them back to Mannheim in pieces."

I gave him a look. Crazy Jake was a fierce fighter, but his moral principals were not a whole lot better than Rabbit's. "I don't fight like that, Jake. You know that. Let's leave the torture and murder of prisoners to Mannheim."

"I thought you said you'd fight the fight on their level, to win."

"There are certain things people like Burroughs do that don't affect the outcome of the fight at all, they're just nasty. That's how I don't want us to get, Jake."

He gave a grunting laugh. "You're the general, General." He walked to the open flap of the tent. "But you said it, this death will scare the hell out of our people."

"We can scare our enemy by fighting like demons in battle," I told him. "What's what we're going to do."

He nodded. "Let's hope that's enough," he said.

Less than twenty-four hours after the soldier brought John Boy's body to me, Mannheim went on the offensive again. Our forward scouts brought news that there was a mass troop movement toward us, and that a tiny village had been overrun on the way.

Mannheim was calling our bluff.

The fat was in the fire.

By the end of that next day, the word was that Mannheim's army was encamped only twenty miles west of our battalion HQ. The land in between had become no-man's land, and there were three or four villages in it. I was sitting at my table desk that evening, studying a topography map of the interim terrain, when Crazy Jake appeared at the flap doorway.

"I got something for you, Rainey."

"Yeah?" I said tiredly. "What is it?"

"There's a guy from one of the villages closest to Mannheim's position. He wants to talk to you. Insisted on seeing the Big General." Jake grinned an irritating grin.

I sighed slightly, and dropped a pencil onto the table. "Hell, bring him in, Jake."

The guy came in, and he was a brawny young Samoan. He carried a bolo machete in his belt and looked as tough as nails. When the Samoans have any size to them, they're about as tough as any people I've seen. They're practically impossible to put down in a brawl.

"You are the General Rainey?" he said, standing with Jake before the table where I sat.

"I'm him," I said.

He looked me over, and I thought I saw disappointment in his square face. I think he expected brass and gold braid. I was wearing a fatigue uniform, with the tunic unbuttoned, showing an ugly hairy chest.

"Well?" I encourage him. "Did you want to tell me something, Mr—?"

"I am called Tanu," he said. "My family lives ina village close to Mannheim's army. It is called Mafili. We have word from a good source that Mannheim will attack your village tomorrow at dawn."

I looked down at my map. He saw me, and came around beside me and put his finger on the place where his village stood. "It is here, General. And Mannheim is here."

Crazy Jake and I exchanged a small grin. I liked the boldness of the man. "Thanks, Tanu," I said.

"We intend to fight Mannheim," Tanu told me. "And he knows that. We have heard of the killings and rape in other villages where Mannheim's criminals have taken over. We would rather all die in resistance than give over our village to him without a struggle."

"I'm glad to hear that," I said.

"We will lose, of course," Tanu went on. "We have a few rifles and pistols. Mannheim can throw a thousand or more automatic weapons against us, and mortars, and flame throwers."

"Flame throwers?" I wondered.

"American. From the last World War. There are

certain of his troops, it is said, that enjoy seeing a man burn to death."

I met his grim look. "Your people are very brave, Tanu."

He nodded. "But they are doomed, General. Unless you come to our defense. Is that why you are here? To save our villages from the wrath of Mannheim?"

"Well," I said slowly. "Individual villages don't count as important in the big picture, Tanu. I'd be extending my forces to strike west that far and so soon."

"We will all die," he said. "Without help."

I looked up at Jake, and he was watching my face closely. He wanted to go, I could see it. "We could be there before Mannheim," he told me quietly, rubbing the scar on his thick-featured face. "We could ambush the hell out of him, Rainey."

I stroked my stubbly chin. "He usually takes two or three assault companies on a mission like this one. Let's assume four for tomorrow. If we matched them, we'd be leaving our defenses down here at battalion headquarters."

"He'd not going to attack here now," Jake said. "He expects to force some more recruits into his ranks from the villages between here and there."

I thought some more, then looked up at Tanu. "Do you know a way to get us there without alerting the whole goddamn countryside? We'd be moving close to a thousand troops."

Tanu nodded. "Yes, General. There is a route that will avoid the villages. I could lead you along it."

I rose from the table, and walked around the tent

some. It would be a real opportunity, if we worked it right.

I turned to Jake. "All right, pass the word down. Companies A through D will be ready to march by midnight. I want to be at Mafili by three a.m."

"You're taking only assault troops," Jake said. "The scream of the Guard."

"That's right. They're the only ones who have a chance of success in this kind of operation. I don't want any field weapons. The village is full of innocent people, people on our side."

Jake frowned. "What the hell, Rainey. The way to win this, to rub their noses, is to wait till they're in, then destroy the village and them with it."

Tanu gave Jake a dark look. "Then we might as well be killed by Mannheim's army," he said in a low voice.

"I agree, Jake," I said. "We'll do it my way. Get cracking, I want every personnel truck in the HQ compound within a half-hour, and you can break out the ammo for the M-16's."

Jake nodded sourly, and started to leave, gesturing for Tanu to follow him. But Tanu stopped him, and turned to me.

"General, please. I would like to go as part of your army. May I enlist tonight, so that I am a soldier in the Civil Guard when I reach my village?"

I grinned at him. "We need every man we can get, Tanu. Jake, arrange for a sergeant's commission for this man, and place him in one of the assault companies."

Jake nodded. "It's done, Rainey."

The next couple of hours were hectic at battalion

HQ. Men that thought they had a night's sleep ahead of them were rousted from their tents and made ready for battle. Guns were cleaned, and ammo distributed. Trucks were lined up in company areas. People in field-weapons companies came and helped, without being asked. Men from rifle companies volunteered to go, and had to be turned down. What I wanted was an enormous SWAT team to go to Mafili, and that's what Jake was getting ready for me. Colonel Tupua came to me and insisted on going with us, but I told him it would be me and Jake and a couple of assault company colonels.

"I need you here, Tupua," I told him. "In case of trouble here."

"I came to fight, General," he complained.

"You'll get to, don't worry," I said.

He fumed some, but I won the argument. That was the advantage of being general. Rank had its privileges. And authority.

It was just past midnight when he moved out, the trucks heading out in single-line convoy, headlights dimmed. I rode in the lead jeep with Tanu sitting beside me. He led us into dirt tracks we could hardly follow, but they kept us away from the populated parts of no-man's land. There was some rocky terrain, and we had a rough ride of it for ten miles or so. Then we finally emerged onto an open plateau where the village sat.

It was a place of less than a thousand people. The huts on the perimeter were nothing more than grass and wattle, but they got more sophisticated as you headed into the center of the village, where most houses and buildings were stucco affairs. There was even some wood. There was one paved street, and the rest were dirt. There were some palm trees and some bougainvillea on stucco walls.

The village had put guards out, to prepare for Mannheim. I stopped the convoy a mile from the village, in case Mannheim had any spies about, and then drove on in with Crazy Jake and Tanu and a couple of riflemen. Tanu got us past the sentries. We went to the house of the village chief, a man who was a member of the *matai* that had elected Awak to office. He was white-haired and weak-looking, but he had resolved to fight Mannheim to the death, and that earned him my respect.

It took just a half-hour with the chief to convince him of the wisdom of placing my troops in every house and building in the village. Within an hour of arrival, my people had entered the village on foot, carrying their automatic rifles and combat knives and grenade-launchers. The villagers looked on wide-eyed as we dispersed ourselves in every nook and cranny in the village, all very quietly, moving in the darkness. About five hundred fighting troops. The rest I had left back at the convoy, and now I sent Jake back there, to disperse them on foot and to make a ring around the village at about five hundred yards, broken up into several platoons of eager fighting men.

By four a.m. we were in place, and the village looked just as it had when we arrived. The streets were black and empty, shutters on houses shut against the night. No sound, no person moving. But inside the houses and central buildings now were

Guard soldiers, crouched and waiting. M-16's ready. Out away from town, behind boulders and bushes, squatted others. Silent. Watching.

I had holed up in the small town hall on its first floor, with a squad of first-line assault soldiers, including Sergeant Tanu, who had asked to be on my personal staff. I think he had ideas of protecting my back. I didn't mind. He was a good man, and I liked having him around.

It was at 4:46, just a short time before dawn, that I got the call over the transceiver from Crazy Jake, out at the perimeter line. I was sitting on a straight chair in the darkness of the big room of the building, with troops all around me, sitting and squatting on the floor.

"*Alpha One, this is Delta Six. We . . . enemy in sight . . . . . . making . . . . . . for him to enter.*"

I rose off the chair. "Set your frequency, Delta Six, and say again."

There was a crackling of static, Then Jake came through clear. "*Alpha One, we have the enemy in sight. He is proceeding toward Mafili in armored vehicles in expected force. We have deployed to allow him a corridor into the village. He has not spotted us yet. He will be on you within minutes.*"

I took a deep breath in, and glanced over at thick-set Tanu. His information had been right. Mannheim was coming, all right.

"Roger, Delta Six. We read you loud and clear. We're ready and waiting. Over and out."

I hurried up some stairs and used a pair of binoculars to stare out past the village limits. And I saw them out there. A double line of armored cars and jeeps, jammed with soldiers. A couple of vehicles had pulled out of convoy. Suddenly I saw a yellow explosion out there and heard the thumping sound of mortar fire, and then came the rocket through the dark air.

I yelled down at those below. "*Incoming mortar fire!*"

I raced back downstairs, and the men there were on their feet, tense now. The mortar shell hit down the street, and banged loudly down there. I looked outside, and saw it had partially destroyed a house. There was more whistling overhead, and more explosions across the small village.

"*Keep down and stay put!*" I commanded my people. "*They're just softening up the village before coming in. Hoping the mortars will take the fight out of them.*"

I was right. In minutes the mortar fire stopped, and then we all heard the grinding of engines as the vehicles of the assault force moved into the village on several of its streets. Still there was no gunfire from inside the house. I had told them. Told them to wait until the whole force was inside the village and was busting into houses. We waited. Suddenly an armored car bursted into the central square, and another one. A loudspeaker on the first one began blaring into the weak light of pre-dawn.

"*Everybody out!*" In Samoan. "*Everybody out of your houses, to surrender to the rebellion! Don't make us come in and pull you out! If you do, we can't gaurantee your safety! Everybody out!*"

We could hear a couple of other loudspeakers blasting out the same kind of message. Mannheim was so arrogant he didn't even want to have to go in and roust the enemy out. He wanted the fight handed to him on a silver platter. I gestured toward my people to move up to the front entrance of the building, by some windows there. They followed orders, and crowded to the front of the big room. Tanu was with them, and a Samoan captain and a young lieutenant. They looked grim and ready. Outside, I could hear gunfire from down one of the side streets, and I knew that our people had made their presence known. It was time to act, before the surprise was gone.

In the square outside, a rebel officer waved toward our building, and a squad came running toward us.

"*All right!*" I yelled. "*Now!*"

My people began firing through the windows, and I yanked the big door open and Tanu and I raked the square with automatic rifle fire. Suddenly throughout the village there was the raucous noise of a fierce firefight, and I could hear soldiers yelling, "*Civil Guard! Civil Guard!*"

They had us outnumbered at that point, though and despite our surprise, they kept firing back, from every street corner and doorway. Machineguns barked out from the armored cars, and I saw a lot of my people go down. They had emerged from the houses now, and the fighting was hand-to-hand on the narrow streets. Several of Mannheim's soldiers had flame throwers, and they advanced behind them down one street after another, spewing flame and setting my soldiers on fire. I saw one of my people run right into the central square, flames roaring from him. He ran for help to another Guard soldier, and set that man afire too. There was a lot of screaming and yelling.

The villagers got into the fight too. I raked the square with my M-16 and knocked two rebels down. One aimed an AK-47 at me, but a villager stepped out of a house nearby and let go with a big revolver, emptying it into the rebel. The rebel was hit in the face, chest, legs. He went down yelling. Tanu was everywhere, but he didn't go very far away from me. I got my transceiver out and yelled into it.

"*All right, Delta Six! Bring them in now! Now!*"

"*Acknowledged, Alpha One. We're coming in!*"

Within minutes our perimeter troops had joined the battle, and Mannheim's people were further surprised. I got a glimpse of Mueller aboard an armored car as it made its way across the central square, blasting out with its machinegun and knocking people down almost indiscriminately. My people, villagers, two of the rebels. Mueller stood invincible atop the vehicle, looking like George Patton in his battle gear. I aimed my rifle and squeezed the trigger, but after a couple of rounds blasted out, my clip was empty. One of the slugs tugged at Mueller's tunic but did not wound him. Then he was gone, down a side street.

"Goddam it!" I swore at myself, replacing the clip.

I grabbed an M-16A1 with a 40mm launcher attached from a nearby corporal, and it was fully baded. I took Tanu and three other men and headed down the side street in the direction Mueller had gone. It would be a real coup to get Mueller, Mannheim's right hand.

Crazy Jake's people had moved into town now. Mannheim's rebels were being squeezed between them and us, and they didn't know where to shoot next. We proceeded down the street. A sniper from a doorway let go on us and one of my men went down, a bullet in his eye. Tanu blasted out at the doorway, and the rebel came screaming out of there, grabbing at his groin and belly. He hit the street and I stepped over his writhing body. At the next alleyway, a rebel shot at me and grazed my left arm. I turned and let go with the M-16A1 and poked little holes in his tunic across his belly and chest. He hung against a wall like he was pasted there, never falling to the ground.

I saw the flash of an armored car down at the next corner, and turned by myself to move through the alleyway, without alerting Tanu or the others. I stepped over a fallen Guard soldier whose left arm was lying across the alley from him, blown off by a grenade. A doorway I passed revealed a fire roaring inside, consuming the building. I could hear the explosions of grenades and small arms coming from every direction, and the acrid odor of gunsmoke hung thick in the morning air now, mixed in with the cloying smell of fresh blood.

It was light now, the sun having just risen from behind distant hills. I proceeded down the alleyway cautiously, able to see well now. I came to the corner of the next street, and stared into the hard, white face of Rabbit Burroughs.

Neither of us said anything, but emotion suddenly blazed across that ugly face. I quickly raised the barrel of the grenade launcher to blow a hole through Rabbit, but in that instant he threw the muzzle of an AK-47 against my weapon and knocked it upward. The grenade was released with an explosion but zoomed past his head and over the building behind him. I squeezed the trigger of the rifle and the hot lead tugged at Rabbit's right ear and collar. He squinted against the deafening clamor at his ear, and grabbed the hot barrel of the rifle, throwing his full weight against me.

"This is it, Rainey, you sonofabitch!" he grated out at me.

"Remember John Boy, you bastard!" I growled back.

Rabbit was not quite as hefty as me, but his arms and legs had wire cables in them, it seemed. He spun around in a death grip, and then were falling to the ground. We hit hard together, rolling around there, scuffling for purchase, grunting and breathing hard. I felt a hard blow to my right arm and I lost the grenade-launcher. I stuck stiff fingers into his ugly face, and tried to blind him. I grazed one eye and he lost one of his contact lenses. We rolled again, and he got a knee into my groin. Suddenly I was groaning on my back and Rabbit was straddling me, pressing his AK-47's muzzle against my chest.

"I warned you, goddamn you," he hissed out like a cobra. "I did the John Boy thing just especially for you. Now it's your turn. Now you pay the piper, jerk!" He grinned down at me crazily, one eye blue and the other pink now. The pink one was tearing down his cheek.

Rabbit's fingers whitened over the trigger of the weapon just as I slammed my arm against its barrel. The gun clatterd deafeningly in my left ear, and hot lead dug up dirt just beside my head, but narrowly missed me. Rabbit lost his balance and fell off me, and I scrambled out away from him and reached for the dropped grenade-launcher. Rabbit was up on his knees now, a desperate look on his lean face. He had lost his cap and a shock of snow-white hair was exposed, to go with the white brows and pink face. He aimed the assault rifle again, and fired. I rolled away and got control of the grenade-launcher, while a couple of shots banged out beside me, hitting the dirt and grazing my thigh. Then Rabbit's clip was empty. As I came up with the launcher, he realized the sudden turn of fate and turned and dived for an open doorway across the narrow alley. I fired after him with a loud explosion, and the grenade shot just over his head and went on through a window in the back end of the small building, exploding beyond it and missing him.

I struggled to my feet and reloaded the launcher from a grenade harness on my battle fatigues. I stepped into the doorway warily, but did not see Rabbit. There was an interior doorway that led to a room on the intersecting street, and I now heard a vehicle start up out there. I ran out onto that street quickly, and Rabbit was kicking up dust behind him in a jeep, racing to get out of there. I aimed to fire after him, but he careened around a corner and out of sight.

"Shit!" I muttered under my breath. "And double shit!"

I had had a good chance at Rabbit, and had lost it. I was goddamn mad at myself. My troops were moving down the street toward me now, looking in doorways, firing into windows.

"*Come on, move!*" I yelled out. "*Don't let them get out!*"

A lot of the town was burning now, from grenades and other fire. I hadn't wanted that, but at least we had saved a lot of lives here so far. I headed down the street Rabbit had driven away on, and my troops followed with a couple of officers. I passed a doorway, and saw a whole family lying on the floor inside. They had been executed by the rebels before we could stop them. There was blood on the walls, on the furniture, and pools of it on the floor.

I heard a tinny bugle and knew it was not ours. Then there was a loud yelling. "*Fall back, fall back! Get out of here!*" It was an Afrikaans accent, and I knew it was Mueller. A jeep was passing me with my people in it, they had commandeered it from the rebels. I jumped in.

"Head down that street up ahead!" I said above the clamor of rifle fire.

We drove down a street off to the left, nearer the edge of the village, and some rebels, looking ragged and scared, retreated ahead of us, firing as they went. A couple of them went down. I looked for Mueller in a retreating jeep, and he wasn't on it. One of my forward people lobbed a grenade, and the jeep just disintegrated before our eyes, rebels and all. Parts of bodies flew through the air, hitting the ground everywhere.

I jumped off the jeep and looked down a side street, the jeep continuing on without me. A couple of noncoms followed me to protect me, but they fell behind, looking into doorways. I turned another corner.

There was Crazy Jake, behind held up against a wall by two rebels. He had been stabbed in the side and blood was running down from his wound, but it did not look like a deep one. Mueller sat atop an armored car with a driver, and had apparently just ordered the two rebels at the wall to hold Jake there. Now Mueller was aiming an AK-47 at Jake. He wanted the pleasure of killing Jake himself, before he retreated out of the village.

"*You picked the wrong side this time, crazy man!*" Mueller yelled at Jake in preparation for shooting him.

Jake saw me now as I raised the grenade-launcher again, and he recognized me immediately. He kept a straight face. The rebels holding him saw me too, and they hesitated for a moment, not knowing quite what to do. Mueller's back was to me, and he not only did not see me, but did not notice the sudden looks of anxiety on his soldiers' faces as I squeezed the trigger on the launcher.

A grenade whistled toward Mueller like a striking snake and bit him in the middle back, punching him hard there. There was an immediate bright-yellow explosion that completely enveloped Mueller and tore him limb from limb. There was almost nothing left of him when the various pieces hit the ground.

The driver was close to Mueller and was killed too in the explosion. Some fragments hit the wall beside Jake and one punched into the face of the captor on his right, the one who still held the bloody knife in his hand that had stabbed into Jake. The guy jerked spasmodically as Jake, his right arm released now, swung a karate chop into the Adam's apple of the other man and killed him instantly.

Crazy Jake and I met at the armored car. He looked a little pale. I had never seen him look pale before. But he took a cigar out, stuck it into his mouth anyway, and grinned at me.

"You saved me goddamn life, Rainey. I don't like to owe anybody."

"You don't owe me," I said. "I wasn't saving you, I was killing Mueller. He was the only one on Mannheim's side that knew strategy."

"I'll forgive you this time," Jake said with a sidewise look.

I glanced down the street. The only rebels in sight now were the lifeless ones on the ground. The others were in headlong flight, and now many were getting away. I figured that at least two-thirds of them had been killed or badly wounded and would never leave the village. We had sprung our trap well. It was Mannheim's first defeat, and it was a bad one for him.

Rainey is here, you sonofabitch, I said to myself, standing there.

I turned and looked more closely at Jake's side wound. "How bad is that?" I said.

"It never entered my body," he said. "It might have cracked a low rib, but that's it."

"I'll get you a litter."

"The hell you will," he growled.

I grinned at Crazy Jake. He was not a bad soldier to have on your side. I was glad I hadn't lost him there.

"Okay, Jake. Let's go check out the casualties."

He headed off down the street, the dead cigar sticking jauntily out of his mouth, holding a hand over his side wound. "Now why didn't I think of that?" he grunted out.

SEVEN

We arrived back at our battalion HQ late that same day. Our people were in a happy mood. We had had casualties too, but we had showed Mannheim what he was up against. There was singing and joking on the trucks on the way back, and I broke rules and allowed some booze in our camp that evening.

We had brought no prisoners back with us. I had no facilities for prisoners. The wounded ones who did not get away were thrown into a jail at the village, and would be tended as best the village could. They did not have our sympathy. They were all scum from the dregs of Samoan society.

Our field hospital was jammed with our own people, though. I made a tour through it that very evening, assessed our damage. There were some who would have to be taken back to Apia and would be lost to us forever. Others would be out of action for some time to come. There were arms and legs blown off, eyes blinded, faces destroyed. None of it was pretty. War and its results had never been pretty or glamorous, not even when it was with spears and bows. The only people who really enjoyed war were born killers, like Mueller and Rabbit, and maybe Crazy Jake. With me it was a way to make a living, the only way I knew. But I wouldn't have been very disappointed if suddenly the world put mercs out of business. I still had the crazy idea that human life is worth something.

Despite all the variety of arms I had managed to acquire for Dr. Awak's new army, we had not really gotten hold of enough ammunition for them, and that was still giving us a disadvantage that we shouldn't have had to go into battle with. I talked to a couple of the wounded soldiers in the hospital tents, and got some complaints from them about it.

"The only reason I got shot, General, was because my M-16 ran dry. I found a vehicle that was supposed to have more ammo, but it was out too. Right after that I got shot."

"I ran out of grenades, General Rainey." This one needed an interpreter to tell me. "The other side had everything they needed. That was very frustrating."

And so it went. I knew I had to go talk to Awak about it before we had any more big confrontations with the rebels. He had promised us more supplies from one of his own sources, and capital to buy them with, but there had been delays. Now we couldn't afford any more delays. We were in it up to our asses.

Late that evening I got my colonel's together, including Tupua and Crazy Jake, and we discussed what had happened at the village of Mafili that morning, and how Mannheim might react to it. We had to be ready for some kind of retaliation. We talked strategy and tactics, and agreed that we should stay on the offensive, if Mannheim gave us the chance to.

At just before midnight we broke up the meeting, and morale seemed high. I had expected resentment among the colonels for my promotion to general, but now I saw none. Our success at Mafili had convinced them that we had good leadership, I guess. Tupua helped my cause too, by always defending me to anybody who had complaints. He stayed in my tent after the others left, along with Crazy Jake and my new Sergeant-aide, Tanu.

"You have clearly demonstrated your strategic abilities to any who had doubts, Rainey," he told me when the four of us were alone. "Now Dr. Awak should be able to stand more opening behind you."

"This is just a beginning, Tupua," I said. "Mannheim knows now what he's up against. He'll be out for real blood now."

"I just want to get the sonofabitch in my sights," Jake said, sprawled on my cot across the room from Tupua and me. "Without Mannheim, this so-called army of his will fall to pieces, and have to go back to mugging people for a living."

Tanu came over to me. He had been angry with me because I had escaped his watchful eye at Mafili and he considered himself my personal bodyguard. But he had gotten over that now, and was being solicitous.

"Would you like another shot of brandy, General?" he asked me.

"No, not tonight, Tanu," I told him. "Why don't

you go get some sleep? We have some long days ahead of us."

He nodded, and left the tent, and Tupua excused himself immediately thereafter. It was only Jake and me there, with our memories of Mafili mixed in with those of similar firefights in other villages, in other remote corners of the world. I sat at my table desk thinking about all of those other ones, and I think Jake was doing the same thing. I wore a bandage on my arm and Jake had a thick one on his lower rib cage, under his tunic. But neither of us were feeling any pain. We had too much brandy in us.

"There must be fifty times like that moment today," he said.

I looked over at him. "Huh?"

"When you blew up Mueller up before he fired that rifle. I can remember so damned many times when I just missed buying the farm, Rainey. By inches or mini-seconds."

"I can recall a couple myself," I admitted. The latest one had been that morning, when Rabbit's clip ran out on him at an inopportune time. He might have killed me if it hadn't.

"What decides who escapes in these little moments and who doesn't?" he wondered.

I looked over at him.

"I mean, other guys have the same thing happen to them and end up with a hole in the head," he went on. "Is it just blind luck?"

"Sometimes it is," I said.

"There sure as hell isn't anybody up there that would want to save the ass of a sonofabitch like me," Jake said, staring at the floor glumly.

I watched his face. "Don't give yourself too much credit. You're probably not quite the sonofabitch you think you are."

"I'm not a frigging Rabbit Burroughs, Rainey."

"I know you're not."

"I'm not that kind of sonofabitch."

"Nobody thinks you are."

"Don't ever think I'm a Rabbit Burroughs, Rainey." He was sounding a little drunk.

I grinned to myself. "I won't, Jake. I promise you."

He sat there, sprawled on my cot, looking as if somebody had insulted him. He was a hard guy to figure out. You couldn't see far into Jake's head. One time he seemed ruthless, almost unprincipled. The next he sat worrying about his image of himself.

"It wouldn't have surprised me if I had bought it today," he finally went on.

"Yeah?"

"I don't expect to make it to fifty," he said. "In fact, I hope I don't."

"Really?" I said.

He looked over at me, and I couldn't tell how drunk he really was. His hard eyes were very serious, his bony, ugly face straight-lined. The scar stood out bold on his cheek.

"It's all downhill from then on anyway, isn't it? I've seen it over and over again. People just waiting around to see what's going to grab at their gut and pull them down onto some hospital bed. Hell, who needs that, Rainey? Isn't it better to go in the heat of battle? A hole in the goddamn head?"

I stared at Jake. I had never heard him talk like

that. "I guess I don't see it that way," I finally told him.

"Yeah? What's your view, General?" He emphasized the title sourly.

I shrugged. "I know people who lasted to ninety and over, with nothing dragging them down till the last moment." I looked past him, remembering. "A fortune-teller in Saigon once told me I've got this longevity thing in my eyes. He read eyes, not palms. He said I might go over a hundred. I guess deep down inside me somewhere that's what I'm gunning for. A little longevity. To get out of this one of these days and maybe set up a little gun shop somewhere and spend some quiet days showing novices how to field-strip a Colt automatic."

"Shit!" Jake scoffed. "You selling guns to old ladies to defend their virginity? Not you, Rainey. You've got this in your blood even more than me. You're going to end up getting your ass shot off in some goddamn jungle somewhere, trying to get some other asshole to keep his frigging head down. Don't give me that longevity shit. You're more like me than you think."

I sat there holding his dark gaze and wondering if he was right. Maybe I would keep on until it was too late to exit with my ass. Maybe, but I hoped not. I sure as hell was not going to count the alternative out, like Jake was doing.

"I think this is getting a little deep for both of us," I said to him. "Unless you want to share that cot with me tonight, I'm going to have to kick you out, Jake. Take the bottle with you if you want it."

He rose unsteadily. "If there's one thing I know,

it's when I've had enough, by God. See you bright and early, General." When he moved past me, he wore a grimace on his heavy features because of the sudden pain in his side. I watched him leave, then rose and undressed. The one man in my army I would hate to lose most now was Jake Murphy.

I'd grown accustomed to his ugly face.

Late the following morning I took a jeep back to Apia. I had to see Awak about supplies that was badly needed, and I couldn't afford any delay in doing it.

Tanu drove me back, and he was an excellent driver. We talked about his home at Mafili, and how grateful he and the villagers were. Tanu's family had survived the firefight, and he looked upon me now like some kind of goddamn savior. I didn't like it, but I didn't want to hurt his feelings. He was like a dog that is blindly faithful to its master. I had never had anybody attach himself to me like that before, and it was embarrassing.

Awak was waiting for our arrival in his grand office at Government House. I came with Tanu and two other armed guards, all of us in battle fatigues, all wearing guns. There were armed guards at Awak's office still too, but now they were my troops under my command. They saluted smarly when I passed them, and I felt the power and respect of my high rank.

Awak and Leilani were both there. I introduced Tanu to the Prime Minister, and Tanu was awed in his presence. Then I told Tanu to wait in the outer office with the other guards. Awak, Leilani, and I sat around Awak's office and exchanged pleasantries.

"You are a hero now in Apia," Awak was saying to me. He sat behind his long desk, looking not quite so wan and pale as he had before. Victory in battle agreed with him. "Your name is on the lips of all of our citizens here."

"It is true, Rainey," Leilani agreed. She looked particularly gorgeous that morning. She wore one of those *cheong sams* with the long slit up the thigh, and had her hair in ringlets all over her forehead and at the sides of her face. It would have been tough to find a more beautiful girl in Samoa. I found that I wanted her, sitting there. The more you got to taste her, the more you wanted. You can't say that about a lot of woman.

But talk about heroism and heroes always makes me impatient. There aren't a whole lot of real heroes. A lot of so-called heroic acts in battle and out of it are nothing more than some poor bastard trying to save his skin. And there are other things that look heroic and aren't. As for me, I can't remember doing anything heroic in my whole goddamn life, and I didn't want to parade around in Samoa as something bigger than life when I wasn't."

"That's all bullshit," I said. "Let's change the subject."

Awak's eyebrows shot upward, surprised at my reaction. "You refuse the gratification of us Samoans for fighting bravely for our cause?" he wondered.

I lit a thin cigar and got it going. "You won't find me posing for any statues, Minister," I said. "What I'm doing, I'm doing for money. Remember? I don't adopt causes, and I don't play hero for anybody. I'm just a guy trying to earn a living, like everybody else. It just happens that what I'm good at is shooting a gun. Don't confuse that with idealism, Minister. Or heroism."

Awak's eyes narrowed down on me. "You are a strange sort of fellow, Rainey. But I like you."

Leilani was smiling. "That makes two of us," she said.

I took the cigar from my mouth and returned the smiles from them. "That part is all right. The feeling is mutual, for both of you. Yes, we did well at Mafili. We rubbed Mannheim's nose in it, and he won't soon forget it. But that was only a beginning. He'll be out for bear now, and he's got an army out there with plenty of equipment and blood in their eyes. He'll be down on us pretty soon now like ticks on a hunting dog, you can bet on it."

Awak's brows had furrowed. "I'm afraid I don't understand all of your English, General. Out for bear? And what are these ticks?"

Leilani laughed lightly. "Rainey just means that Mannheim will attack soon, and in force."

Awak nodded. "But that is good, isn't it? Let him come, we have a real army now. The sooner the better, since the Parliament is now clamoring for a quick victory and an end to the fighting."

I made a face. "I've heard that song before," I said sourly. "Yes, we want a fight just as much as Mannheim does. But we have to have that equipment you promised us, Minister. We're running short already, and we've just begun. When is your supplier going to come through for us?"

Awak shrugged. "I called just yesterday. They say they can have the military supplies here next week."

I shook my head. "Not good enough. I want them here within forty-eight hours. Mannheim could catch us short. If he does, it could be a disaster."

"But Rainey. They tell me that next week is the soonest—"

"Call them back," I said. "Tell them I want that stuff within forty-eight hours or the deal is off. Tell them that if they comply, there will be a ten-percent bonus in it for them."

Awak sat there, taken aback by my insistence. "I'm not sure they will agree, even on those terms."

"They will," I said. "If they don't, I'll contact some people I know. Let them know there's a competitive supplier in the picture. Tell them to haul ass or they're out."

"Well—" Awak managed.

"We'll call them, Rainey," Leilani put in for him. "I think they will come through, with the offer of a bonus."

"Yes, we will call," Awak said hesitantly. He was not accustomed to an aggressive leadership style. He didn't wear the mantle comfortably.

"The next thing is," I went on, "I hear you gave Mataafa another job."

"Why, yes," Awak said. "We had pressure on us, Rainey. The *matai* called me to account. It was a compromise, you see. I appointed Mataafa to a lesser administrative post to appease the opposition. Surely you're aware of the give and take in politics."

"Mataafa is no damned good," I said.

"Rainey, I've taken over Mataafa's duties here," Leilani told me. That was a surprise to me. "I'm Father's deputy now. The *matai* has approved.

Mataafa has no chance of returning to this post. Actually, he is doing a good job where we placed him. He is a fact of life we must all live with, Rainey. Including you."

I stuck the cigar into my mouth and regarded her grimly. It seemed that she and Awak would never learn who could be trusted and who couldn't. "It's your country," I said.

She smiled nicely. "Well put, Rainey," she said. "And so true."

"If I get the feeling there are people here that are working against my victory in the field, though, in any way," I said to her, slowly, "I'll drop this war like a hot potato and leave you to fight out your own battles. That's a solemn promise."

The room was quiet for a long moment, then Awak cleared his throat and spoke up. "General, my daughter and I are one hundred percent behind you. We have been from the beginning, and we will be until this thing is finished. You can count on that."

"I'm glad to hear that," I said.

"Of course, there are a few pro-Mataafa members of Parliament who would like nothing more than to see you go down in defeat," Leilani admitted. "And people who backed General Tofa. But they are a very small minority."

I rose from the chair they had seated me in. I walked over to Awak's desk and stubbed the cigar out in a cut-glass ashtray there. "Well, if we don't get those supplies, those dissenters may just have a big party coming up," I said to them. "Don't fail us, Minister."

"I will do my very best, Rainey," he told me.

I had some other business to finish in the capital,

so I decided to stay over that night with Tanu. On the way out of Awak's office I hinted to Leilani that I'd like to see her that evening, but surprisingly she didn't pick up on it. I had never gone to bed with a Deputy Prime Minister before, and wanted to feel her out while I felt her up. But whereas Leilani had always been the aggressor between us before, now she played it coy, it seemed. I had to wonder about her change of manner toward me, after our other intimacies, but I didn't push it.

That afternoon Awak called me at garrison HQ, where my general's banner now flew above the compound because of my presence there, and informed me that we would get our supplies the next day. The bonus offer had moved his suppliers to action, that and the threat of cutting them loose.

I felt better with that news. After supper at HQ, I took Tanu out with me that evening to the Fiji Bar.

The Fiji Bar was on the old waterfront, set among whorehouses, tattoo parlors, and gyp joints. It was one of those end-of-the-world places with sawdust on the floor, ceiling fans overhead, and a stink of beer and sweat mixed on the warm air. We could have gone to a hotel bar, but I hoped there would be less chance of anyone recognizing me in the Fiji. I was wrong.

We made a genuine effort to mix in. We wore fatigues stripped of any insignia whatever, and we left our sidearms at HQ. We sat at a table in a far corner and kept a low profile. It didn't help. About mid-evening a tough young punk walked over to our table and stared hard at me.

"Hey! Ain't you that big-ass general they hired to whip Mannheim's butt?"

Tanu and I looked up at him. He looked Samoan, but with some Anglo in him. He must have spent some time in the States at one time, because he spoke almost without an accent.

Tanu gave him a tough look. "Get lost, mister."

The guy ignored him. He turned to some ugly-looking men at the bar. "Hey, look at what we got here! A real big-ass hero, for Christ's sake!"

Tanu rose to tell the guy off, but I motioned to him. "It's okay, Tanu." He sat back down slowly, as one by one three other men, all drinking buddies of the first one, it seemed, wandered over to stare at me. The one had had come first was brawny and bow-legged. Among the other three, one had a club foot, a second one was lean and completely bald, and the third was very Samoan, with the broadest nose I had ever seen. They were all dirty-looking street punks, looking for trouble. They all had a couple of drinks in them, I guessed.

"By the holy gods!" Clubfoot muttered. "I have never seen a real general before!"

"Where are your stars, General?" Baldy said in a grating voice.

Broadnose grunted his words out. "This general is a mercenary. He wears silver dollars on his lapels, is it not true, General?"

The first one there, Bowleg, laughed a dirty laugh. "Man, you don't look much like a general, without no stars on your shoulders."

"You are disturbing the general's privacy," Tanu growled at them. "Go drink your swill and leave us to ourselves."

Broadnose moved up closer to the table. "Who the hell are you, Samoan flunky?"

Tanu rose again, angry, his dark eyes flashing. But I intervened. "This is Sergeant Tanu," I said easily. "A soldier fighting for your freedom."

Bowleg moved up on me. "Freedom? Is that what you tell them? That you're giving us freedom? Hell, I'm free! Any of you guys need these jerks to give you your freedom?"

"Hell, no," Clubfoot said in a low voice.

"We hear you shot General Tofa with your own gun," Bowleg went on. "That true, General?"

I hesitated. "Yeah," I nodded.

Broadnose scoffed. "That is the way he gives people their freedom. He shoots them and releases them from this awful life!" Some guttural laughter.

"I warn you, don't talk to the general this way!" Tanu said a little loudly.

"Shut up," Bowleg said quietly.

The few other people in the bar had turned their attention to us now, and I didn't like the spotlight we were in. I rose too. "You'll have to excuse us," I said. "It's getting late."

Broadnose barred my way, and Baldy came over to join him. Bowleg and Clubfoot were standing nearer Tanu.

"Tofa had friends in this town, American General. Did you know that?"

"How lucky for him," I said. "I could have guessed they'd be like you."

"Where's that gun you murdered Tofa with?" Bowleg said, the one who spoke like an American.

"I've still got it," I told him.

"But not with you," Bowleg grinned.

"Not with me," I admitted.

"That is too bad," Broadnose said. "Because you

might just have to pay a price for your killing, American. Before you leave here tonight."

"Oh?" I said.

Bowleg and Broadnose exchanged a look. "Yeah," Bowleg said. "I think it's time for a little accounting."

"Get out of our way!" Tanu said loudly.

But they had no intention of letting us leave peacefully, and I had known that from the beginning. I heard the slick sliding of metal on metal, and suddenly both Broadnose and Bowleg had blades in their hands. Baldy reached behind his waist and came up with a kind of blackjack. Clubfoot fumbled in his shirt and a short length of iron pipe slid into his hand.

"Oh, shit," I muttered.

"Why you—" Tanu growled. He went for Bowleg. Bowleg slashed out with the knife, and cut Tanu across the left arm, and then they went down together, Tanu hitting and punching at the other man. They almost knocked Clubfoot over as they went. He swung the pipe at Tanu's head and missed. Instead, it hit Bowleg over the right ear and cracked his skull loudly. He landed on top of Tanu, a shudder passing through his body from the blow.

Now Broadnose was on me, him and Baldy. Broadnose came like a freight train, big and husky, stabbing quickly into my midsection with the siletto-type knife he held in his right hand. I took a step to the side and the knife blade ripped my tunic loudly, grazing my belly underneath. I swung a karate chop at his neck, and connected at the base of his skull. His neck snapped under the impact, his head whiplashing, and he fell up against the wall beside me.

But Baldy was on me too. I felt the blackjack thud against my shoulder and neck, and I grunted out in sudden pain. I fell against the wall just as Broad-nose slid down it, eyes glazing over. Baldy struck out with the blackjack again. I ducked aside, and the weapon thumped hard against the wall beside my head. If the blow had struck, it would have smashed my skull like a melon. I kicked up into Baldy's groin, and he screamed loudly. I punched stiffened fingers into his chest, over his heart, and he sucked air in, gagging, his face going gray. I made a pirouette and swung the back of my hand against the bridge of his nose. There was the further cracking of bone in the room, and Baldy crashed over our table and took it and two chairs down with him.

I turned. Tanu had gotten out from under the dead figure of Bowleg, but now Clubfoot stood over him, about to swing his weapon down onto Tanu's broad face to crush it. I kicked out at Clubfoot's bad leg and broke his knee at the joint.

He yelled and fell beside Tanu. I moved in and he grabbed the club pipe to bust my shins with it. I beat him. I kicked him hard in the face, mashing his cheek and nose and sending splinters of bone into his brain. He jumped spasmodically, as if he were getting up off the floor of his own volition. Then he collapsed into a pile there.

Tanu rose slowly. He had done well for a peaceful man. "Are you okay?" I said.

Tanu looked at his bloody left arm. "The cut is not deep, General. But you are hurt also."

There was minimal blood on my tunic from the belly scratch. It was my shoulder that hurt like hell. I moved my right arm around, and felt it more. "Hell, I'm all right."

A heavy bartender came over. "You . . . killed all of them," he mumbed in awe.

I looked down at the floor. Actually, we had only killed three. Bowleg bought it because of Clubfoot's clumsiness. But Tanu had contributed, by trying to move away from the blow.

"Yeah," I said. "It looks that way." I reached into a pocket and peeled off some bills and laid them on the nearest corpse. "There. That's for the drinks and the entertainment. You ought to be able to get help with the clean-up with the extra money. The next time you see me in here, try to keep your other customers under control."

We left then, with the bartender looking slack-jawed after us.

It was almost midnight when we got back to the garrison barracks, where we were to sleep that night. The sentries on duty saluted sharply when they recognized me, and then stared hard after us as we drove through the gate, because we looked like we had just come off a battleground.

Tanu insisted on putting two guards outside my sleeping quarters when I went to bed, and I let him win the argument. He was becoming too protective of me, but I didn't want to hurt his feelings. He wanted all requests to see me to come through him, and I didn't mind that either. I tried to get through to Crazy Jake out at battalion headquarters before I hit the sack, but he had gone out with a night patrol and I couldn't reach him.

I went to bed at about one, and at three a.m. I was awakened by a soft knocking at my bedroom door. It was Tanu, and he had somebody with him.

"What the hell, Tanu," I said. "You know it's the middle of the goddamn night?"

"I understand, General, and I apologize for waking you," he told me. "But Colonel Matautu came to see you, and he says it is urgent that he see you right now."

I looked beyond Tanu and saw the familiar face of Matautu, the retired officer who had informed on Tofa. "Oh, Matautu," I said. "Hell, come on in, Colonel."

He and Tanu both came in and we sat down around my private bedroom and stared at each other in the overhead light. I had been deep asleep and was finding it hard to wake up.

"You have my humble apologies, General Rainey," Matautu began. "But they have me followed. I got here without being seen only because it is the middle of the night. I had no choice."

"May I get you a drink, Colonel?" Tanu offered.

Matautu shook his head. He looked even more frail than the last time I saw him, and his hair looked whiter. The expensive shirt he wore hung on him loosely, as if it belonged to a much bigger man. "No, thank you. My time is severely limited."

"What brings you here in the middle of the night, Matautu?" I wondered. "Is everything all right with you?"

"With me, no," he said. "I am followed day and night by people I have never seen before, and I feel my life is in danger. But that is not why I came to you."

"No?" I said.

He looked around the room, as if somehow there might be some way for an unseen enemy to be spying on him. "It is about Mataafa."

"Oh," I said. "Yes, I know. He's been made Deputy Minister for Public Works."

"No, that is not it, General," Matautu said emphatically. "It seems that Tofa had friends in the Ministry of Public Works. Friends who have not given up on the idea of forming a coalition with Mannheim against the current government."

"I see," I said.

"No, you don't General. You see, Mataafa has gone to Mannheim."

I frowned, and leaned forward on a straight chair. "What?"

"That same relative who spoke to me before knows it for a fact," Matautu insisted. "It came to him from the same nephew. Mataafa met with Mannheim on the north coast, in a tent camp there, and spoke with him for four hours. This was just three days ago."

"I'll be damned!" I swore under my breath.

"It is believed that Mataafa has made a pledge of assistance to Mannheim," Matautu said. "He is not as formidable an ally of the rebellion as Tofa, but he can be used by Mannheim in various ways."

"That sonofabitch," I grunted. "I should have shot him too."

"Indeed," Matautu agreed with me.

"I can arrange that now for you, General," Tanu offered.

I glanced at my thickset sergeant. Tanu was as

loyal as they came. He was an asset to the cause.

"I don't know," I said slowly. "Maybe we could do ourselves some good by just watching him for a while."

"I have already taken the liberty of doing so, for several days," Matautu advised me. "Mataafa has had private conferences with some interesting people. Two subordinates in the Ministry of Public Works. A captain in the local garrison of the Guard. Dr. Awak's daughter."

I narrowed my eyes down on him, unbelieving. "Leilani?" I said.

He nodded. "Of course, the meetings could have been innocent on her part, I have no hard evidence against her. It is just that they have been so careful to meet privately."

I thought back on my intimacies with Awak's beautiful daughter, who was now Deputy Prime Minister, and realized that she did have a strong ambition burning inside her. But I never thought she had the capacity to betray her own father, especially considering what could happen to him if a man like Mannheim came to power. Suddenly, though, her new official power in the government seemed dangerous to me.

I looked over at elderly Matautu. "I'm going to leave Tanu here in Apia with you for a while," I told him. "Who is watching Mataafa for you?"

Matautu grinned. "Just a boy. A boy I would trust with my life. He is only sixteen, General, but he is very skillful at this kind of thing."

I nodded to him. "All right. Colonel, how would you like to operate a small counterespionage cell for me here in Apia for a short time?"

Matautu smiled. "That would suit me fine, General."

"Just you and the boy and Tanu," I said. "I'd like the boy to keep track of Leilani, and we'll put Tanu on Mataafa. We might be able to learn the depth of this fifth column here. I think it's probably just getting started, so we'll be able to nip it in the bud."

"General, I wish to return to battalion HQ with you," Tanu said to me. "I am a soldier, not a spy."

I had to grin inside me. Up to a few days ago, he had been a farmer. "The duty I'm putting you on is soldier's duty, Tanu. It will be more dangerous than open battle. The things you find out could be more important than winning a big battle in the field."

"It is true, my boy," Matautu said.

Tanu was convinced. "Well, If it is really dangerous duty," he said.

"It is, believe me," I assured him.

A few minutes later, Matautu was gone. But my middle-of-the-night interruption was not quite over. Tanu had left my room for only five minutes when he was back knocking on the door again. I went and opened it with a sour face. "Now what, Tanu?"

"I'm sorry, General. There is a messenger."

"A messenger? Who from?"

"He says he comes from headquarters, sir. Colonel Jake sent him."

Now I saw the disheveled soldier for the first time, looking tired and out of breath. I stepped out into the corrider and looked him over. He was one of us, all right. "What is it, Corporal?" I asked him.

"It is about Mafili, General."

Tanu and I exchanged glances. "Yes?" I said.

"Colonel Murphy received word just a couple of hours ago. The small garrison you left at Mafili. It has been attacked and wiped out by Mannheim's rebels."

A deep frown grew on my grim face. Tanu caught his breath in, thinking of his people in his home village.

"It is reported, sir, that some of our soldiers were captured alive." The courier hesitated. "Each one was killed slowly, General. Their screams were heard by the villagers all through the evening hours. Now Mannheim's officers are trying to find villagers who may have aided us in our attack there. They will be executed."

"Holy God," Tanu murmured.

I looked at his sallow face, and knew what he was going through. I turned away from him, thinking for a moment. Between Mannheim and me, we had brought hell to Mafili three times over. I had to wonder whether our victory there was worth it. I let a deep breath out. "Get the jeep ready, Tanu. I'm leaving for the front line immediately."

EIGHT

The men I had left at Mafili were few in number. Mannheim had not really hurt our army, not in terms of physical strength. But he had done something to morale. You could smell it when you entered that tent encampment that night, like you can smell carrion when you get within miles of a battlefield. I didn't like the smell of it. It was the smell of defeatism, of stagnation. To the average soldier, it seemed that Mannheim's retaking of Mafili had wiped out their victory there. That was not true, of course. We had bitten a big chunk out of Mannheim's forces in that battle, and what he had done in return was minimal. But it had had its effect on the guts of my troops. They were down.

You have to understand that this was not a professional army that Crazy Jake and Tupua and I were leading. They were just very ordinary civilians with minimal training. They reacted very emotionally to any setback, no matter how small.

"They're like a bunch of little kids, for Christ's

sake," Jake told me the next dawn as we sat out in front of my HQ tent with Colonel Tupua, assessing what our next move ought to be. "They all think they're going to be captured and tortured. They're scared."

"Don't think too harshly of them," Tupua said to Jake. Tupua sat reclining back on a lawn chair, with a topographical map on his legs. He thought we were ready to strike out at Mannheim now in full force, to force a real confrontation.

"Where are we now, Tupua?" I asked, still staring upward. "Where will we meet Mannheim?"

"Our scouts say that Mannheim has moved his troops forward, to the north of here," Tupua said. "He is missing all along this front, General. Readying for battle. His men number almost as many as ours. And he is better supplied."

"Not as of later today," I told him. "We're getting the stuff we ordered, finally. If Mannheim is ready to duke it out, we'll be there."

"I just hope the men will fight," Tupua said.

I rose from my chair. "They'll fight," I told him. "Jake, I want you to round up every officer and noncom at battalion HQ. Assemble them at the corral, I'm going to remind them what we're out here for."

Jake rose and grinned. "Right on, Rainey."

Tupua rose too, and I turned to him. "Tupua, I want you to receive our supplies later today, and do a quick inventory for me. I want to know what we've got to fight with."

"It shall be done, General."

Within an hour I stood before several hundred men at a fenced-in enclosure used for horses and mules. The men assembled outside that fence, in rows, and I stood on a jeep and talked to them.

"*We're fighting something here besides rebel soldiers,*" I said to them over a rigged-up loud-speaker that echoed and bounced across the open area. "*We're fighting fear, because of those reports from Mafili. Maybe some of you are afraid. If you are, I won't blame you. I will blame you if you show that fear to the men, or encourage theirs in any way. Every one of you is a leader. It's up to you to set an example for the rest of them. Turn that fear you see into anger, damn it! When I heard what had happened to our people at Mafili, I was mad, I can tell you! I'm still mad, goddamn it! Aren't you mad, too, all of you in command here?*"

There was a scattered response.

"*I didn't hear you!*" I yelled out.

"*Yes, we're mad, General!*" came the chorus back.

"*Good! I want you to spread that anger to our troops! Turn all that fear and depression into an emotion that will act for us! Can you do that?*"

There was a loud yelling assent.

"*Okay. Now listen to me. We're getting our supplies today, and we're going to be ready to go on with this war. And there's something else I want you to share with the troops. I'm sending a message to Mannheim!*"

Crazy Jake, sitting beside me in the jeep, took his cigar out of his mouth and stared at me, waiting.

"*I'm telling him that this fear tactic is never one-sided. I'm not going to lower us to his level and give my people carte blanche from here on out. There will be no torturing in any outfit of mine. But I'm serving notice on the rebels today: from here on to the end of this, the Civil Guard will take no prisoners in battle!*"

There was silence over the compound. Crazy Jake let a grin crawl into his thick face.

"*That will be our answer to Malifi,*" I told them. "*No prisoners!*"

There was a resounding echo from our officers. "*No prisoners!*"

"*Spread the word!*" I commanded them. "*Spread the anger! From now on, the rebels can fear the Civil Guard!*"

There was a lot of cheering and yelling, and I hoped that that new zeal would spread downward through the ranks, and quickly.

By mid-afternoon, it seemed that my hope had been vindicated. There was a new spirit among the troops, a revitalization. They had quit thinking of themselves as victims, and had begun regarding themselves as warriors. They knew that, when my message reached Mannheim, a new aura would hang over them, to the enemy. That aura would be danger. They had become a force that the rebels had to worry over, think about, reckon with. A rebel either had to fight and win against us or be killed. There was no middle ground for him. I realized that that could work against us in isolated instances, because a man would fight harder if he knew he had no hope of survival upon surrender. But generally, it would make the rebels reluctant to continue on with a fight if it started going against them. It would put the idea of flight into their heads, flight before the possibility of total annihilation. I hoped it would also foster desertion in Mannheim's ranks. I had seen it happen in armies I fought in.

I knew a big battle was forming. Mannheim wanted it, and I wanted it. But I sat there at HQ that afternoon wishing there were some way to bloody Mannheim's nose before the Big Fight. I didn't like going into a big field battle with Mafili the last thing that had occurred between our armies.

Then, later that day, I heard about a company of Mannheim's hard-core rebels that was moving from the coast toward Mannheim's main battle line with supplies for his troops.

There would be fifty miles of open country they would cross before gaining the protection of Mannheim's lines, and we would not overextend ourselves to meet them in that open no-man's land.

I liked it.

When Jake came in to report that our supplies had arrived, I told him about my idea to intercept the supply company.

"I want to go," he said eagerly. He was already bored from HQ duty.

"Jake, I've run a hundred ambushes like this one. I'm going, myself. I want to make sure Mannheim learns a lesson from this he won't soon forget."

"Then let me go with you," Jake countered. "I've run almost a hundred ambushes. In all kinds of terrain."

"I know it, Jake. But I need you here. And your rib is still healing."

Jake stared hard at me. "Come on, Rainey!" He tore open his tunic and exposed a bandage on his side. With another ripping motion he stripped the bandage from his flesh, making me wince.

Underneath was a red, healing scar and some stain of blood. "I've been meaning to take this thing off all day. Can't you see I'm healed? It's a goddamn scratch, for Christ's sake! I'm coming, Rainey!" he added defiantly.

I sighed, and looked at the wound. It wasn't healed, but I knew Jake was a tough sonofabitch. "Shit, okay, Jake. We'll both go. But I don't want you risking your ass unnecessarily there. I'm going to need you."

Jake grinned. "You make it or you don't," he said. "It's all a Parker Brothers game anyway, Rainey. All jou-jou and rau-rau and witch-dancing. I thought you knew that."

I squinted down on Jake. There were things going on in that head that I would never fathom. "Just try to be a little careful," I told him, sounding suddenly like a goddamn parent.

"Oh, incidentally," he told me. "I think Tupua told you there was one survivor of the last Mafili thing, one of our private soldiers. Tupua wondered about that, and had the guy questioned by a sergeant who knows his business."

"And?" I said.

Jake made a sound in his throat. "The guy's a turncoat. Has a brother in Mannheim's HQ company. He got a message out of Mafili to Mannheim, telling the rebels how few people we had there, and how best to take the village back."

"He admitted all of that?" I said.

"That's what Tupua says."

"How was the information gotten?"

Jake shrugged. "Just a knocking around, I guess.

No hardcore hurting." He added, "Like Mannheim would do."

"Is this general information?" I said. "Among the troops?"

Jake nodded. "Yeah. He's outside right now, under guard. In case you wanted to see him."

I sighed. "Okay. Get him in here."

The man came in with his guard. Jake pulled him over in front of the table I used for a desk. Jake gave me his name, which I found almost unpronouncable. I looked him over. He was just a kid, with an innocent kid's face.

"Why did you do it, Private?" I asked him.

He licked dry lips. "There is a man, he is a soldier for Mannheim. I knew him in Apia. He sneaked into Mafili disguised as a local farmer. He found me and asked me questions about our strength there."

"That doesn't tell me why you did it," I said.

He averted his gaze for a moment. "He and I shared a jail cell in Apia two years ago. While in the cell, I confessed a crime to him. One the authorities knew nothing about."

"I see." I shook my head slowly.

"If I had not told him everything I knew, he would have reported me to the authorities through a cousin in Apia. I would have been taken from here and thrown into jail again."

"Probably," I said. "What kind of crime did you confess to?"

He hesitated again. "There was this twelve-year-old girl."

He gave me a look and stopped. Jake and I exchanged sour looks. "You would have been thrown into jail," I agreed with him.

His face brightened slightly. "Then you understand, General?"

I regarded him soberly, then turned to Crazy Jake. "Who was it that pried all this loose for us?"

"One of my sergeants," Jake said. "A Samoan in K Company."

"Promote him to officer rank," I said.

Jake nodded.

"And who would be responsible for recruiting this man?" I went on.

"I think it would be some lieutenant in the Apia garrison, under Tupua's command originally."

"Sort him out and discharge him," I said.

Jake arched the thick brows. "Okay."

"You understand, General, yes?" the private said now doubtfully.

I looked up at him. "You caused the massacre of a fine garrison to save yourself from prison, Private." I took a deep breath in and let it all out. "I don't require my men to believe in a cause, or have high moral principals. I'm not sure I believe in the notion of treason generally. I don't care whether you come to me for political ideals or for money. But once you join my side, I expect you to fight to win. There isn't any room for toleration of betrayal."

He licked lthe lips again.

I glanced at Jake. "Get six riflemen together from B Company, and take him to the corral. Spread the word about what's happening. Do it as soon as you can get the people together."

The private's jaw fell open. "You will shoot me? Murder me in cold blood?"

"You will be executed by an assigned firing squad, soldier," I told him. "I'm sure you know the penalty when you spilled your guts at Mafili."

His innocent face grew a very different look, an ugly one. "You American swine! You are just as they say you are, a filthy killer! I spit on you!" He spat onto my table desk, and spittle slicked over a topographical map there. "You are dirt under Mannheim's feet, hired killer! You will die at his hand!"

"Take him away, guard," I said.

The guard almost jerked the private off his feet as he moved him out of the tent. When I turned back to Crazy Jake, he was grinning a crazy grin.

"The bastard had guts. It's too bad."

"Yeah," I said. "Tell me when it's over."

"I'll get right at it."

"And then let's get some equipment ready for our move out. That supply column of Mannheim's is going to be at Pago Pago at about mid-morning tomorrow. I want us to be there."

"We will be," Jake assured me.

That night passed slowly. The execution of the private brought morale down some again. Not because of the sentence I handed down, but because no soldier likes to think there are betrayers amongst his people. It makes you think. That's what I was doing that night, instead of sleeping. Crazy Jake had moved into my tent and spent half the night cleaning that Webley Mark IV of his. All good soldiers keep their weapons clean, but Jake had a thing about it. He treated that revolver like a goddamn baby. The damn thing was so oiled up it almost glowed in the dark. When Jake was sober, he was good with it too. He had a fast draw that would have made John Wesley Hardin sit up and take notice. I can still see him oiling that Webley up that night, and then carefully replacing those stubby-looking .38 cartridges that could blow a hole right through a man.

At the next dawn I took Jake and several other officers and two platoons of good men armed with automatic weapons and made off for Pago Pass in rocky, hilly country not more than twenty miles from our battalion HQ.

We got there at eight, with the sun already making the morning warm. We stopped just on the north side of the low pass between rocky outcroppings. We had had to make a wide detour around Mannheim's main lines, a kind of end run to avoid his big army. Now we situated ourselves on either side of the rutted track that we knew Mannheim's supply column had to travel on to get past us. We took up positions behind rocks and boulders and scrawny trees. Besides the small arms, we had brought two .50-caliber M85C machine guns and a 90-mm recoilless rifle and a Dragon antitank missile-launcher.

This time we were going to give Mannheim something to think about.

This time we were ready.

We waited. The sun climbed higher in the eastern sky, eating the color off the horizon and concentrating it in one glare above our heads. We sweated and waited some more. I was on the north side of the road manning the Dragon missile-launcher, and Jake was opposite me with his half of the strike force. He and a lieutenant were ready with the recoilless rifle. Down the line a way on either side the machineguns were set up and manned by soldiers who knew how to use them effectively.

It got to be 9:30, then 9:40. At 9:43 we heard the rumble of heavy equipment coming along the road.

I gave the signal for the troops to keep down and wait. We all disappeared behind our cover.

Because we were on high ground, I had a view almost immediately of the approaching column. They came up a gradual rise toward us, six vehicles in all. There was a lead jeep, then four trucks, then a jeep bringing up the rear. Each of the jeeps was loaded with troops, armed to the teeth. I figured at least one of the trucks also carried guard troops. The others would be jammed with ammunition, guns, and equipment.

They drew to within a hundred yards, growling up the incline. I could see the expressions on the broad faces of the Samoan rebels in the lead jeep. One of them was laughing at some joke. I got a buzzing on the transceiver I held in my left hand.

It was from our scout at the forward post down the hill. "*Rear six-by carries twenty personnel, Charlie One. All armed with Russian Kalashnikovs. The other trucks are tarped over. Do you copy?*"

I pressed a button. "I read you loud and clear, Charlie Two. Prepare for assault signal."

They came up to thirty yards. Ten. Then they were passing between us. A radio was playing in the lead jeep. We could hear the rebels talking among themselves. Unaware of what was about to happen. I leveled the Dragon at the first truck beyond the jeep. When it went off, that would be the signal for the attack.

I fired the missile.

There was a dull explosion and a whooshing sound

as the Dragon missile snaked to its target, hissing like a cobra. When it reached the truck, there was a deafening, bright-yellow eruption there that wracked the still morning air. The truck jumped off the roadway and part of it just disintegrated, and debris was thrown everywhere.

Now, suddenly, there was hell on that small road. The column halted one vehicle at a time and men began yelling excitedly as more explosions ripped the morning from the first truck, ammo going off inside as fire ravaged it. Our nearest machinegun cut loose on the lead jeep, and rebels grabbed at their chests and toppled to the ground. The other machinegun was already raking the rear jeep, and fire was coming back at them. At the last truck, rebels were now piling out of it and trying to find out what was happening to them. A couple of them started running wildly away, but were cut down by machinegun fire.

Jake and his partner at the recoilless rifle boomed out another shot, and it hit the second truck. Again there was a bright explosion, this one louder even than the one from the Dragon missile, and the truck disappeared in a puff of white smoke and a chain of further explosions. Shrapnel came flying at us, and I saw one of my people hit in the face. He screamed and died there quickly.

Only seconds had elapsed. I reloaded the Dragon with a second missile and fired again, at the third truck. It was the one with the remaining supplies. The missile whistled toward its target and again hit on center. The driver had already scrambled out, but the truck exploded with such force that he was caught in it. He was set afire and went running into the rocks. One of my people brought him down with automatic-rifle fire.

All the rebels were now out of that fourth truck and were returning fire to us now, crouched and kneeling on track. Two more of my people were hit. The sergeant beside me, only two feet away, was hit in the neck and a fountain of crimson spurted from his jugular. I dropped the Dragon, picked up an M-1A1, and launched a grenade into the kneeling rebels. Another violent explosion, and three of them were picked up and thrown off the track. Others were falling with every second, and there were only a few left. They fired back blindly and wildly, with smoke billowing around them on the road track. I stood up with the grenade-launcher hanging loosely at my side.

"*No prisoners!*" I yelled.

Crazy Jake rose now and echoed the call. "*No prisoners!*"

A rebel turned and tried to run, and was hit in the low spine. He whiplashed and fell. Another one got up and held his hands high, throwing his gun down. He was shot in the head. Now there were only two left. One got up and bravely walked into our fire, shooting toward us with raking gunfire. He was torn almost in two by machinegun fire. The last live rebel turned and dived for a ditch, and three different guns caught him in mid-air. His body was jerked and punched around as it fell to the ground, then it hit hard, in an awkward heap, a bloody mess from head to foot.

There was a short burst of additional gunfire, ten it was still.

Out on the roadway, flames licked at the three trucks and smoke billowed high into the warm air. Mangled bodies were everywhere. Crazy Jake walked out onto the track, aimed the Webley at a still-moving rebel, and shot him in the head. Then it was over.

We all came out onto the track with Jake, and just stared at the destruction we had wrought. There were no cheers of victory. No joking and laughing. Those corpses on the ground did not provoke laughter in sane men. But we had shown Mannheim something. We had hurt him, and we had shown him.

It was a part payment for what he had done at Mafili.

Crazy Jake came up to me. He already had a cigar stuck in his ugly face. He looked very satisfied with himself.

"You want an exact body count?" he asked me.

I shook my head. "No. We know what we did. Let's get the hell out of here before Mannheim hears about this."

Jake nodded, and moved off toward our silent troops.

NINE

Our success at Pago Pass lifted morale back up again, and I figured our troops were ready to fight. During our absence at the ambush, a large patrol of ours had met some of Mannheim's rebels out in no-man's-land, and we had whipped them there too. That also helped our *esprit.*

The rumor was that Mannheim's people had been shocked by the two victories, and that there had been a few desertions. But we knew that wouldn't faze Mannheim. He was ready for a big showdown between our armies, and so was I.

The afternoon of our arrival back from Pago Pass, I got my several colonels together and told them that we would be planning an all-out attack in the next few days, and I wanted input from all of them. They knew the terrain better than me, and they knew Samoans. We had a long briefing in my HQ tent, and when it was over, Tupua and Crazy Jake stayed on to have a word with me.

"Tupua has some information for you that we

thought we ought to keep confidential, Rainey," Jake told me.

We were sitting around the tent in a close knot. Tupua had become a valued confidant of Jake and me, and we had a lot of respect for his ability as a soldier. He looked over at me. We had poured drinks and were sipping at some brandy.

"I didn't want to mention this until the three of us could be alone," Tupua told me. "As you know, we received our supplies yesterday, and once again it was not as much as expected. "Well, I think we know why."

"I don't know if I want to hear this," I said.

"To begin at the beginning," Tupua went on, "the fifth column you set up in Mataafa's viper's next is no more."

My face went grim, and I felt myself clutch at my shot glass. "What?" I said slowly.

"Matautu is dead," Tupua told me. "The boy he hired is dead. Your Sergeant Tanu is hanging onto life by a slender thread at Apia General Hospital."

"What the hell!" I growled, rising from my chair.

"Matautu was found at his residence. He was so perforated with stab wounds that he was almost unrecognizable. The boy was found in an alleyway near his house, with his throat cut."

"Sonofabitch," I said in a low voice.

"Sergeant Tanu was found outside a bar where Mataafa had spent some time that evening. He also was left for dead. He had been shot three times with an apparently silenced gun. He is in intensive care and not expected to survive."

"Sonofabitch," I repeated. I remembered telling Tanu that the duty I was putting him on was soldier's duty, that it was dangerous. But I had not expected this.

"You were right about Mataafa," Jake told me.

"It is true," Tupua said. "Tanu has talked to one of our loyal Apia garrison officers, and that officer relayed the information to us. Tanu says that Mataafa and Leilani Awak meet regularly in secretive rendezvous, and the dead boy overheard them talking. The word is that it is Leilani who is in charge, not Mataafa. It was she who managed to have about half our supplies withheld from us in the field here."

"Goddamn!" I grated out, punching my fist into a nearby file cabinet and making it rattle.

Tupua waited a moment for me to turn back to him. "Including, Tanu says, four Dragon antitank missile-launchers, a half-dozen recoilless rifles, and an unexpected armored combat vehicle."

It was obvious that Crazy Jake did not know all of this that Tupua was now telling. I saw anger grow on his face as it was growing on mine.

"You bedded that bitch!" he snapped at me.

I nodded tiredly. "Don't remind me," I said heavily.

"There would be no need for these heavier weapons in our Apia garrison," Tupua went on. "It is apparent that Leilani does not want us to succeed in the field, General. It is even possible that those weapons and supplies could wind up in the hands of Mannheim."

"They may already be on their way to him," I said. I looked over at Tupua. "What about the Apia garrison? Do you think it's still loyal to us?"

Tupua shrugged in his uniform. "Who can say?" he said.

"Don't even think of going back there, Rainey," Jake said, reading my mind. "Without this army with you."

I turned to him. " have to, Jake. I've got a little war going on now within the big war. I have to win the little one first, or there won't be much point in fighting the bigger one. I have to see Tanu. If they haven't killed him. Then I have to see Awak."

"Dr. Awak is sick again, General," Tupua said to me. "Sick and incompetent to perform his official duties. But he is too proud to admit it. His daughter is duping him and he doesn't know it."

"Well, somebody has to tell him," I said. "Jake, get a jeep and driver ready for me. I'm going to drive back to Apia immediately."

"Don't be a goddamn jerk, Rainey!" Jake said angrily. "You and a driver? Into that hornet's nest?"

"For Christ's sake, do what I tell you!" I yelled at Jake. I was shook up by these sudden events, and in no mood to argue.

He glared at me for a long moment. "Okay. You and a driver. Right on, General." He turned and left briskly, not giving me a second look.

I turned to Tupua. "If I don't get back here, you're in charge, Tupua. You know what has to be done. It's going to be a fight to the death."

"I know, Rainey."

Less than a half-hour later, I was gone.

It didn't take long to get to Apia. When my driver and I arrived there, the streets looked quite deserted. It was beginning to look like there was a war going on. I drove right to the capital barracks where my offices were located. The barracks were heavily guarded, but the guards recognized me immediately and we drove on in. The armored combat vehicle that was supposed to have been sent to me was sitting idle in the compound. I swore under my breath as we stopped there, but was glad it hadn't been sent off to Mannheim by some devious means. That also meant, probably, that the rest of my supplies were here in the capital somewhere.

There was a lot of clicking of heels and saluting as my driver and I entered the headquarters building. The interior of the place bristled with armed men, and a couple of them looked sidewise at me with sober looks. I went directly to the office of the colonel I had put in charge, a man named Sese.

"What in the hell is going on here, Colonel?" I demanded as soon as I found him in his paneled office.

He rose with a worried look, then tried to smile. He was a heavy, out-of-condition officer who had been highly placed in the police before the reorganization. "General Rainey. How surprising it is to see you back in Apia. We just heard about your great victory at Pago Pass."

"Why wasn't my equipment and supplies sent out to me?" I insisted, my blood boiling now. "You had direct orders, Sese. From me."

He nodded quickly. "Of course, General. But when Miss Awak countermanded those orders, I had to presume you had been involved in the decision. After all, she is the Deputy Minister."

"You got orders from Leilani to hold all this stuff here?" I said. I wanted to hear it from him.

"Why, yes," he said innocently. "I thought surely you knew, General." But I thought the innocence was feigned.

"Goddamn it, when I give you an order, you check with me before you go against it," I said in a hard voice. "Do you hear that loud and clear, Colonel?"

His voice went flat. "Yes. I hear you, General Rainey. But my new orders came from a Deputy Prime Minister, who outranks you, I'm sure you'll agree. I had every right to assume that she had cleared the order with you. If she felt that was necessary." He said the last with just a slight touch of acidity.

I walked over to him and stood with my face in his. "You said you hear me, but you don't, damn you. Place yourself under house arrest until further notice. I'm relieving you of command."

He face me coolly. "I'm not sure you can do that, General. Under the circumstances."

I scowled at him. "What circumstances, you bastard?"

"Perhaps you haven't heard. There is talk of replacing you as comnmander of the army."

The scowl on my face deepened. "Oh, yeah? Who's doing the talking, Colonel? You?"

"On the contrary. It is spoken in the highest circles."

"That means Leilani and that goddamn Mataafa," I said.

"I believe those were two names that were mentioned."

"I pointed my finger into his face. "Remove

yourself from command, Colonel. If I hear you haven't, I'll court-martial you."

"I shall make a note to myself," he said.

I left there in a huff. Jake had been right, this was getting hairy. I got back in my jeep and told my driver to take me to the hospital. When I got there, I went directly to see Tanu.

He was still in intensive care, and there was no guard on him. I got on a phone and called headquarters and avoided talking to Sese. I ordered a contingent of guards to the hospital, and when I identified myself, I was promised that six men would be sent over immediately. I wondered.

When I went in to see Tanu, he was the only one in the small white room. He was conscious, and a big grin appeared on his square face when he saw me.

"General Rainey. I hoped you might come."

I sat down beside his bed. A nurse came up to me and leaned over Tanu to check a hose to his left arm. "You can stay only a short time, General," she told me.

"I know," I said.

She left and I turned to Tanu. "I'm glad to see you alive, my friend," I told him.

He made a slight shrug. He had been hit in the stomach, the high chest, and the side. He had lost a lot of blood, and had had to have two separate operations to repair his insides. He should have died with that many bullets in him, but he was a tough egg.

"Matautu was not so lucky, General. Or the boy. But we gave you important information, did you get it?"

I nodded. "I wanted to make sure I got it straight, though."

He repeated what Tupua had told me, with few additions. "It seems there is a move to betray our cause and turn over the government to Mannheim," Tanu said.

"There always was," I told him. "The mistake I made was in thinking I had ended it by shooting Tofa. I thought Mataafa was harmless. And I never suspected Leilani Awak. I've been pretty goddamn dumb."

"It is dangerous for you in Apia, General," Tanu told me. "You don't know who your friends are."

"I know. I stand in the way of Leilani now. At first she thought she would rise to power through me, when I licked Mannheim. But then Mataafa must have gotten to her, and showed her how much easier this way would be. And how much more likely she will be to retain power under Mannheim than a government her father and I would set up."

"What will you do, General Rainey?"

"I was hired to fight and win a war," I said. "Until Awak himself tells me he doesn't want that any more, that's exactly what I intend to do."

"You need me out there," he said. "I must be well soon so that I may be with you."

I touched his arm. "All you have to do is recover from your wounds. Take your time, Tanu. We'll take care of the war. I'm putting a guard on you around the clock in case our enemies decide to try again to kill you."

"I will be all right, General."

Just as I was leaving, a few minutes later, the

armed guard arrived. I broke them up into two groups and put three men on duty immediately, the other group to relieve them in twelve-hour shifts until further notice.

My next stop was Government House.

Awak was not in. He had fallen seriously ill and was at home under doctor's care. I went to Leilani's new, plush offices, bullied my way past a secretary, and found her there in a meeting with Tupuola Mataafa.

They both rose from their chairs upon my bursting into the room. Mataafa looked a little scared, but Leilani was cool as a cool cucumber.

"Well. It's you, Rainey!" Leilani said pleasantly. "What a nice surprise!"

I gave Mataafa a hard look, and went over to Leilani's expensive teak desk with its cut-glass ashtrays and silver accoutrements.

"Did you know when you came out to visit me at battalion HQ?" I said in a low voice. "Did you know when I took you to my goddamn bed that you intended to betray me?"

She put a hurt look on her beautiful face. "Let's not be emotional, Rainey. How can I betray you? This is after all my country, not yours."

Mataafa laughed. "Well put, my dear."

I pointed a finger at him. "Get that pimp out of here."

"What?" he said, acting outraged.

"Get him out of here or I'll shoot him," I said, speaking only to Leilani.

The scared look came back into his oily face. "This is inexcusable!" he blustered.

Leilani held my hard gaze. "It's all right, Tupuola. I will speak with you later. You're excused."

I knew in that moment that Leilani was in charge, as Tupua had guessed. She was a much stronger person than Mataafa. He was only dangerous because of his deviousness and duplicity.

Mataafa stuck out his chin. "Very well. If you insist, Minister. I will be in my office if you need me."

"I'll call you," Leilani assured him.

A moment later he was gone. I relaxed some and sat on a corner of Leilani's desk.

"You probably withheld supplies and equipment from me," I started out. "You've made a deal with Mannheim, haven't you? Just like Tofa before you?"

She shrugged beautifully. She was wearing a skin-tight *cheong-sam* dress with a slit up the thigh, and her hair was drawn back tight, with dark curls at the sides of her chiseled face.

"It's time to talk turkey, Rainey, as you Americans often say. I come to recruit you because I thought Mannheim could be easily beaten with an organized government army. Now I see that I was wrong. He's very strong, Rainey. Yes, I think I've arranged a coalition with him that will work for the good of the country and avoid bloodshed."

"Bullshit," I said. "You've been offered power by Mannheim that your father will never give you, because he knows you'd abuse it."

She smiled. "My father has some backward notions, as do many of the *matai.* They want me out of this job as soon as they can find a male replacement. They will never give me any real authority in this government, nor will my father. Mannheim will. There, is that honest enough for you? Does that make me a villain?"

"You take on the character of the company you keep, Leilani. You must know what it will be like if Mannheim owns this place. You used to tell me."

"I can be a positive influence on him, Rainey," she said. "Don't worry so much about it, it isn't like you."

"Mannheim will eat you alive," I said to her. "He'll make you his whore. Do you think he'll be willing to share his power with anybody? Let alone a woman?"

"Yes, I do," she told me. She sat back down, and let the slit show her long thigh. "Listen to me, Rainey. I want you to join forces with us. You can retain command if that's what you want. But acknowledge the authority of the coalition leadership. You can be a great asset to us. Mannheim holds no grudges against you, I've spoken with him about you."

I shook my head sidewise. "There are some people I just couldn't work for, Leilani. One of them is Mannheim. And I'm beginning to suspect a second one is you."

She let a scowl mar her soft features. "This is your chance to get out from under a bad situation, Rainey. Don't be a fool about it. You've always been smart about money all your life. Don't get dumb now. You're not going to beat Mannheim, there are forces joining up with him every day. You might as well jump onto the winning side. Isn't that what your career is all about, Rainey? Winning fights?"

"Not at any cost," I told her. I rose off the desk. "Your father and the *matai* apparently still want me to try to save Samoa from Mannheim, and that's what I expect to do until they decide to stop my pay."

She rose again too. "Don't try to stand alone, Rainey. It isn't a position that becomes you."

"I guess that's a threat," I said.

"Take it as you like."

"I'll tell you what I'm taking. I'm taking that armored car from the garrison compound, and all the other supplies that belong to our army, and I'm moving it all to battalion HQ in the field."

"You can't do that," she objected. "You'll leave the capital undefended if you strip it of that equipment."

"Undefended?" I said. "Your army is out there between Mannheim and the capital for the express purpose of defending the capital from his attack, Leilani. I'll deploy military equipment as I see fit to get the job done."

"Then I must exercise my authority to prohibit you from taking that equipment," she said to me harshly.

"As of this moment, I don't recognize your authority," I told her. I turned to leave.

"You'll be sorry, Rainey!" she called after me.

"We'll see," I said

My driver and I left the building immediately, but as it turned out, Leilani was faster than us. As we came down the wide steps of Government House, a jeep pulled up full of soldiers. One of them was Colonel Sese. They all piled out of the jeep and surrounded us, pointing assault rifles at us. Sese came up to me holding a Taurus Magnum aimed at my midsection.

"Well, General Rainey," he said with an oily smile. "I'm sorry to announce to you that it is you who is under arrest."

My driver was infuriated. "How dare you! Nobody arrests our general!" He started to go for his revolver on his hip, and I stopped him before they killed him.

"It's all right, Corporal," I said easily. "Colonel Sese, I don't recognize your authority to arrest me. I'm commander of this army and this garrison."

"I am here under higher authority," he said. "The authority of the Prime Ministry."

"Dr. Awak didn't send you," I said.

"His daughter is acting on his behalf during his illness," Sese said to me. "I suggest you don't make an issue of it here, General. If you do, we will be obligated to shoot you on the spot."

I studied the faces of his men, and knew they had been brainwashed by him. They would follow his orders. I also knew that if I allowed myself to be taken away by him, I would be quietly executed in some dark cell somewhere and never see the light of day again. I was just wondering what to do when I heard the roar of engines coming into the wide square. In a brief moment, several jeeps came squealing to a halt all around us. There were six of them, and they were jammed with combat troops from my battalion. The lead jeep carried my general's stars on the fender, and the banner of my HQ company fluttered from an antenna.

Soldiers piled out of the vehicles, armed to the teeth, and drew a large circle around the four men

Sese had with him. One of the newcomers was Crazy Jake Murphy, and I had never been happier to see that ugly, hard face. He came up with an assault rifle pointing muzzle skyward, an ammo belt across his chest, and a cigar stuck into his mouth.

Sese and his few men looked suddenly very scared. Sese quickly lowered the Taurus Magnum to his side.

"Well, Rainey," Jake said in his tough voice. "Looks like we got here just in time to give you a ride back to camp. You got some kind of trouble here?"

He knew exactly what kind of trouble I had, and that was why he had come in to Apia against my orders. But this was Jake's way of giving me the needle.

I grinned. "It seems that Colonel Sese here was about to arrest me," I said. "Without proper authority."

Sese swallowed hard. "General, I was merely carrying out—"

"Shut up, you!" Jake said. He stuck the muzzle of the rifle up under Sese's chin, and jerked the sidearm from his grasp. Crazy Jake had never had any respect for epaulets on a man's shoulders.

At an order from Jake, my battalion men yanked the assault rifles from the guards Sese had brought with him, and they all looked terrified now.

"You were sent on a fool's mission, Colonel," I said to Sese. "Even if you had managed to kill me, there are too many good men out there at battalion HQ who won't just throw their arms down because you or Leilani order them to. They intend to fight for their island."

"That's the frigging truth," Jake agreed.

"Arrest these four men," I said to a subordinate officer who had come with Jake. "Take them back to the garrison barracks for court-martial."

Sese looked relieved that I had not included him in the arrest order. The captain I had spoken to nodded, and my people began herding the Apia men into one of the jeeps.

"What I would like to explain, General," Sese began now, with more confidence, "is that—"

"Thanks for coming, Jake," I said.

"Any time," Jake said. "Anyway, I owed you one."

"I want you to come with me to Awak. I want to get things in order here before I get on with our real war."

"Got you," Jake said.

"General—" Sese was insisting.

"And, oh yes," I said. "Shoot him." I threw a thumb toward Sese.

Jake had lowered the rifle. He nodded now, raised the rifle as Sese's eyes saucered in surprise, and squeezed the trigger of the gun casually, as if he were swatting a mosquito. The gun popped off two quick rounds, and they caught Sese in the center chest. He jumped off his feet and was thrown ont the high steps behind him. He died there in just seconds, staring at me as if I had just played some terrible practical joke on him.

The men who were being herded into the jeep had turned and were staring at Sese horrified. Now my people prodded them on into the vehicle.

Jake took a long drag on the cigar, as if he had

already forgotten the figure on the concrete steps. "Now. Where does this Prime Minister of yours live?" he said.

TEN

Prime Minister Awak reclined on the fancy bed, propped up by three pillows, looking like the death scene in some Grade-B movie. He hardly looked like the same man who had hired me just a short while ago. His hair was uncombed, he had a light stubble of beard, and his face was as pale as a gull's wing. He tried to smile at me, but it didn't work. He only succeeded in making himself look sicker.

"I've had a relapse, Rainey," he croaked at me. His voice sounded like it had been dredged up out of a sewer drain. "I am sorry to have to meet you like this."

"You're looking quite well, Minister," I lied. "I hear you're on your way to recovery." I sat on a straight chair beside him. A white-frocked nurse had just left the room and waited outside in a hallway now with Crazy Jake. We were in Awak's private residence on the outskirts of Apia, and had had to bull our way past guards placed outside by Leilani and Mataafa.

"That is an optimistic appraisal," Awak said, in the grating voice. "My lungs are gone, General. It is just a matter of time for me, I suspect. How is our little war progressing?"

I took a deep breath in. In the brief silence, I could hear the rattling breath of Awak as he sucked air in through the damaged lungs. "Before I answer that, I want to tell you something, Dr. Awak. I'm still your employee, general's stars or not. Any time you decide you don't want me on your payroll any longer, that's it. I'll be gone, and I won't look back. Do you understand?"

He arched graying brows. "Of course, Rainey."

I leaned forward on the chair. "Leilani doesn't want to save Samoa from Mannheim," I said slowly and clearly. "She's made a deal with him."

His face seemed to go even whiter. "What?"

"It's true. Mataafa and Mannheim have corrupted her with promises of power. She's your daughter and I know you've placed your confidence in her, or you wouldn't have given her an official post. But we have hard evidence that we'll submit to you. Leilani no longer wants me around. She tried to have me arrested just less than an hour ago, but my troops intervened."

He let a rattling breath out, his gray face sagging with dismay. "I should have known. I had hints, General. One doesn't want to admit certain things about one's own daughter."

"If you just say the word, Dr. Awak, I'll bow out of this and let Leilani handle things the way she sees fit. Of course, when Mannheim's thugs move in, her life won't be worth a Samoan dollar."

"I'm well aware of that."

"If I stay, I'll want authority to run this thing my way until we've won or lost, subject only to your approval. Leilani and Mataafa will have to be placed under house arrest until this is over. Some of their friends will have to be thrown into our garrison prison. I'll bring several of my loyal officers into Apia to take command of the garrison here while I'm in the field. Those are my conditions for staying on, Minister."

There was another long silence in the bedroom. The only sounds were Awak's wheezing and a ticking wall clock across the room. Finally he looked over at me with resolve in his thin face.

"Do what you have to, to win this war," he said. "To save the people of Western Samoa from Mannheim's kind of world."

I rose, and nodded. "I hoped you'd say that, Minister."

"I'll make some calls," he said. "To let my cabinet know what you're doing, and that it's with my authority."

"I appreciate that." I walked across the room, then turned back to him. "I'm also placing Apia under martial law until this is finished," I added. "There will be no midnight meetings of Leilani's and Mataafa's friends to revive this thing with Mannheim. I want to be free to concentrate my efforts on winning the war in the field."

"I agree," Awak grated out. He then coughed violently into a handkerchief.

"Take care of yourself, Minister," I told him.

He tried to smile again, and it still didn't work. "I seem to have little choice, Rainey."

When I left Awak's house I didn't immediately

leave Apia. I sent Jake and some soldiers to arrest Leilani and Mataafa first. Mataafa had a couple of bodyguards with him, and one of them tried to defend him and was killed. Mataafa was taken to garrison headquarters under guard, yelling that we would all be executed when Mannheim's troops marched into Apia. I arrested Leilani myself, and she made no effort to resist. She just gave me a hard, cold look as Jake directed guards to keep her under confinement at her own apartment. Jake then went about business of calling in some officers from the field, rounding up some of Mataafa's military and other friends, and announcing martial law on the local radio stations.

When the others left Leilani's apartment, I stayed on for a few minutes. We stood in the center of her art-deco living room with her staring out through glass doors that overlooked a tropical view of the city.

"I didn't think you'd do this to me, Rainey," she said.

"You tried to do it to me."

"I wouldn't have let them hurt you," she told me.

I went over to her. "Something's got hold of you, Leilani. But that's your problem now. Yours and your father's. I'd guess if we win this he'll go easy on you. Maybe ship you off to Sidney or L.A. with a big bank account to draw on."

She turned to me, and we were quite close. I could smell the good smell of her, and she was even more beautiful than ever to me. "If you should win this war," she said, "it still wouldn't be too late for us to form a partnership, Rainey."

"No?" I said.

"Father is living on borrowed time. This country is going to need leadership desperately, Rainey. You may not think much of my moral values, but I have certain abilities in politics. You and I could run Western Samoa together. You could know a life you've never dreamt was possible. You could live like a king, Rainey. You can't go on fighting wars all of your life, you know."

I grinned. "King and Queen of the islands?" I said. "Rainey the First? His and her royal majesties?"

"Something like that."

I shook my head. "You don't give up, do you, Leilani? No, I don't see myself as a ruling monarch. Or any kind of politico. A man ought to keep doing what he's good at until he can't anymore. Then I'll probably end up training recruits in some Latin banana republic, getting drunk on bad liquor, and contracting syphilis with some whore that can't speak English."

"Is that what you really want?" she wondered.

I thought for a moment. "Yeah. I guess it is."

She shrugged. "Then if you beat Mannheim, it seems you'll go on getting shot at ad infinitum, and I'll be sent off to bask on the beaches of Southern California. It sounds awful, Rainey."

"Not for me, honey," I said. I walked to the closed door and then turned back to her. "Also, don't forget. Until this is over, you and I are on the opposite sides of something. Don't try to cross me again, Leilani. Or you may never see that beach in California."

"You wouldn't hurt me, Rainey," she said.

I pointed a finger at her. "Don't count on it," I said.

By the time I left Apia later that day, things appeared to be under control finally. A half-dozen of my better officers had been recalled to the city to take charge there and make sure Leilani and Mataafa were kept under tight guard. In addition, a curfew had been put in effect for that evening. Jake and I drove back at dusk in a small convoy, taking the new equipment and armored car with us.

We arrived at the front-line HQ at dark, and when the troops heard that we had brought the needed equipment, there was some celebrating. I didn't put a squelch on it because I knew they needed the release. I also knew that if there was going to be a big confrontation coming soon, this might be their last time to live it up before going into battle.

The next morning was a bright, sunny day and I felt good about things. I had put down the trouble in Apia that had been brewing behind my back, and now I had a war to fight against a capable opponent. Who could ask for anything more, in my line of work? The new equipment was disbursed, our armored vehicle was readied for combat, and the men seemed ready.

At just before noon I held a general review on our parade ground, and was pleased with what I saw. We had turned a bunch of green civilians and cops into an army. Now, over the next few days, while my scouts kept an eye on Mannheim's troop movements, I would confer with my colonels about what our first offensive move would be.

Not long after lunch in the officers' mess tent,

with Crazy Jake and me still sitting there talking about Mannheim's possible offensive capabilities, Tupua came in and sat down beside us at the trestle table. The three of us were alone, but Tupua lowered his deep voice anyway.

"A messenger just came from Mannheim," he said in a very conspiratorial tone.

Jake and I exchanged looks. "Really?" I said.

"Maybe he wants to surrender to us," Jake offered sourly.

Tupua smiled, acknowledging the joke. "I'm afraid not, Colonel. He wants to meet personally with you, Rainey."

I grunted, thinking. "Did he say what for?"

"There was no indication. He offers to meet with you at a point called Rurutu Rock, halfway through the no-man's land that separates our two armies, and only about six miles from here."

"When?" I asked.

"Tomorrow. At mid-morning. He suggested ten."

"He already knows about Leilani and Mataafa," Crazy Jake said.

I nodded. "I'm sure he does."

"He will come in a jeep with a driver and two other armed men," Tupua went on. "You must do the same, no other vehicles or men. He will provide a canvas cover for you to meet under, and it will be set up by meeting time. He will come under a white flag."

Jake looked over at me. "What's the point?" he said.

I shrugged. "Maybe he wants to avoid a fight. Maybe I can talk him into flying out of here and taking his guns with him."

"Maybe the moon is made of green cheese," Jake suggested.

"I don't see what's to be lost," I said.

"This could be a very dangerous undertaking to you personally, Rainey," Tupua said urgently.

"You're damned right," Jake agreed. "It could be a goddamn death trap!"

I sat there. "Maybe the whole country is a death trap for us," I said to him finally. "You and I may find our boot hill here. But isn't that the chance we take every time we strap on a gun for somebody else?"

"That's not the same," Jake grumbled. "Listen to me, Rainey. You've got this bastard right where you want him. That's why he's coming to you with his goddamn hat in his hand. You've got nothing to gain and everything to lose in a lonely meeting with him. I say, tell him to stuff it. Let him hear from you the way you know how to talk best. With guns."

Tupua nodded. "I tend to agree with Colonel Murphy," he said.

I paused. "First of all, don't underestimate Mannheim's strength. I don't see any hat in his hand. What I do see is an army out there waiting to kill. If there's one chance in a hundred that I can avoid some of the killing that's to come by meeting privately with Mannheim, I've got to take the chance. You two see that, I hope."

"There isn't any way to avoid killing. Not when you're dealing with a sonofabitch like Mannheim," Crazy Jake told me.

"Again, I agree with the colonel," Tupua said.

I sat there thinking. "I'm sorry, you two. But I

have to go. Tupua, arrange everything. Hand-pick my driver and guards."

"I'll drive you," Jake said quickly.

"The hell you will," I said.

He rose and stood over me menacingly. "I'm going, goddamn it."

I had to marvel at Crazy Jake. He had turned into an almost likable guy since hiring on here, a soldier that actually cared about the people he fought with. It was a goddamn miracle.

"You saved my ass in Apia," I told him. "You don't owe me a thing, Jake, remember?"

"Shit, I'm not talking about any of that!" he said loudly. "If you get yourself killed out there with Mannheim, who the hell is going to general this war?"

I rose and looked into his thick face with its long scar. "If something happens to me out there, Samoa is going to need you and Tupua to get it out of this mess. I couldn't risk you, Jake. It's basic strategy right out of the manual."

"Screw the manual," he offered.

"I'm sorry, Jake," I said. "Tupua, please get my car ready."

Tupua nodded reluctantly. "It shall be done, General."

Actually, I didn't get much sleep that night. I had to agree that Crazy Jake was right, I was taking a chance going out there to meet with a cunning, conniving bastard like Mannheim. But if I went ahead and attacked him and let all that killing take place, and then found out later that he really had wanted some kind of honorable truce that we could live with, I would have a hard time living with it. I had no real choice, not if I wanted to be a responsible commander. I had to presume something could come of a talk with the enemy, until such time as it was obvious I could accomplish nothing with talk. Then the guns could explode.

The following morning was another beautiful one, and we were under way by 9:30. I took the three men suggested by Mannheim, and two of them were armed with M-16's. My driver wore a Taurus Magnum sidearm, and I carried my Browning Mark I on my hip.

We drove that six miles very carefully and warily. At the feet of my two guards in the back seat lay a 90-mm recoilless rifle that I had put aboard the jeep, covered with a tarpaulin. I hoped that Mannheim would not insist on searching the vehicle. The larger weapon could give us a small edge if Mannheim had death in mind for us.

There was no sign of an ambush. In about twenty minutes we crested a small rise and saw the outcropping known as Rurutu Rock.

There was a jeep already parked near the outcropping. We stopped at my command and studied the situation. A canvas fly had been set up to protect from the sun, and there were some chairs and a table set up under it. Mannheim was sitting at the table, and Rabbit Burroughs was with him. Two sentries were already alerted to our arrival, and were pointing toward us.

I could see no other vehicles about, and there was little place for them to hide at that site. My driver glanced over at me. "It seems safe at the moment, General."

I nodded. "All right. Let's go on in."

We drove on up to the other vehicle, slowly and warily. My men in the rear seat had their weapons at ready. But Mannheim came out like a long-lost brother to welcome us.

"Rainey! What a pleasure to meet with you again! I thought you would come.

I got out of the jeep slowly. Mannheim's sentries and my guard eyed each other with mistrust. My driver turned the engine off and the sudden silence pounded on my ears. Rabbit Burroughs came out from under the canvas, squinting his blue-over-pink eyes into the glare of morning sun. I remembered what he had done to John Boy, and a bile rose into me momentarily.

"When a man wants to talk with me, I usually give him the courtesy of listening," I replied to Mannheim.

"I knew you were a gentleman, Rainey, and a man I could trust to sit down like a civilized man and listen to reason. After all, we're all the same kind of men here, aren't we?"

I gave him a look, and glanced past him at Rabbit. "Not really," I said to him.

He ignored the disagreement. "Come, sit under our canvas," he invited me. "We have brandy and bourbon and gin. I know you won't turn down a good drink, Rainey."

I walked over to Rabbit, and stared hard into those subhuman eyes for a long moment. He grinned an evil grin at me. His white skin was reddened from exposure to the tropical sun. "Rainey likes bourbon. That right, Rainey? Or have you changed to sherry, since your romance with that little whore of Awak's?"

I wanted to draw my Browning automatic and put a piece of hot lead into Rabbit's grinning face. But that would defeat the purpose of my coming. I had to bide my time. "Make it brandy," I said to Mannheim, without replying directly to Rabbit.

I went and sat at the table, and Mannheim joined me there. Rabbit poured the three of us a drink, and my driver came and watched the proceedings carefully. My other people stood at the jeep, not far away. Despite the pleasant conversation, the air bristled with tension.

Rabbit gave Manheim and me our drinks, but did not join us. He went and stood a short distance away, while Mannheim settled himself comfortably onto a canvas chair.

"Well, Rainey. Some things have happened since we last met, yes?" Mannheim said in his German accent. His dark hair was slicked back neatly, and his prominent nose was slightly sunburned. He wore khakis with no rank insignia, like me.

"Yes, some things have," I agreed.

"It did not surprise me that you retaliated on our supply convoy, after our attack on Mafili," he told me. "That was a clever ambush, by the way. You know your tactics well, Rainey."

"I learned from experts," I said.

"It also did not really surprise me that Leilani Awak failed in her attempt to neutralize you. I understand you have her under arrest now."

"Her and your friend Mataafa," I said with satisfaction.

He laughed good-naturedly. "I should have

known that fool would be no good to me. He is a coward also, as well as a fool. Did you have him shot?"

"Not yet," I said.

He laughed again. "It would be good riddance. Mataafa is just the opposite of men like you and me, Rainey. He is a parasite, always depending on the accomplishments of others to see him through. He always needs alliances with stronger men. You and I don't, do we?"

"You tell me," I said.

He grinned more broadly. He was my buddy, my comrade-in-arms but from the other side of the battle line, a fellow man of the world. He was the biggest goddamn liar since Hitler.

"I don't have to tell you, Rainey. You understand the way men are and the way the world is. The spoils go to the strong, hasn't it always been so?"

I swigged some brandy, and looked over at Rabbit where he stood leaning against a pole that held up the canvas fly. A man who could hire Rabbit and put up with him had to be a real bastard. But I still hadn't given up some small hope that there could be an avoidance of bloodshed. A small breeze flapped the canvas over our heads. One of my men turned and spat on the ground, then eyed Rabbit with a hard look.

"I guess that's been the usual rule," I said.

"Of course it has. I knew you would recognize that simple fact. And it will always be so, Rainey. Men like you and me will always be the ones who are in charge, the ones who must show others the way. It is a great responsibility, of course, but we are not the kind to turn our backs on responsibility. We like a challenge, Rainey, men like you and me."

I turned and caught his mellow gaze. I had thought there would be an offer of some sort of compromise by now. "Is that why you got me out here, Mannheim?" I said deliberately. "To list the ways you think we're alike?"

He swigged down the whole of a shot glass of gin, then set the glass down carefully on the table. "That is merely a preamble to what we will discuss momentarily. We will not speak further of us, Rainey. We will talk now of you only."

I gave him a look, and turned away.

"You have fought in every corner of the world," he went on. "I bothered to look into your background, Rainey. You've taken on jobs that few Third World leaders could have handled. Field commander. Advisor. Secret agent. Confidant. Courier. Negotiator. You have done it all, Rainey, and done it well. You have always assumed the posture that it is fighting on the line that you like best, developing tactics for small units of fighting men and carrying out those tactics. But you and I both know you're ready to move up from all that now. Look at how capably you're leading an entire army at the moment. Why, with a little luck, you could even beat us!" He laughed that gusty laugh again, and Rabbit turned and gave him a narrow look.

"With a little luck," I agreed.

"You see how we understand each other?" he went on. "We talk the same language, Rainey! I still don't see why you didn't join us in the first place, instead of going on salary for Awak. Even at this point, I could offer you a substantial raise in pay."

He hesitated, watching my face. "No thanks, Mannheim," I said.

He nodded. "I understand. You've reached the point in your career at which you don't want to work under other military leaders. You want to carry the whole load yourself, and reap all the glory and profit. A laudable motive, of course."

"It isn't the money, Mannheim," I said.

"It is only one of several motives, I know," he said. He leaned toward me. "Primarily, it is power. But we don't talk about that, do we?"

I just stared at him. The more he talked, the less I liked him. And I had disliked him an awful lot in the beginning.

"I've already been offered a partnership in power, Mannheim," I told him. "By your former allies."

He grinned. "I thought Leilani might try that. Of course, you realized she couldn't deliver on her offer."

"If I beat you she can," I said to him.

He kept the grin. "Yes, but in that event, you would probably not need her. If you allies yourself with me, Rainey, there would be no question of the future. The government would be ours. We would move our combined army into Apia and begin our work of ruling these islands. I see a joint leadership, or perhaps a triumvirate, with you and me picking a third member of a very powerful *troika.*"

"And you'd make sure that the third man was one who would always vote with you," I smiled nicely.

This time Mannheim didn't smile. "I'm sure you could take care of yourself in matters political, Rainey. What I'm suggesting to you is a very real and very substantial. And there is absolutely nothing to stand in our way, when we combine forces."

The warm breeze moved the canvas again. I knew that there were mercs who would have jumped at Mannheim's offer, even knowing that they would have to deal with him later. But I wasn't one of them. The thought of doing anything with Mannheim was a downer to me.

"You're right, of course," I began. He smiled. "There would be nothing that could stand in our way if we combined forces. We could do with these people in Samoa exactly whatever we wanted. Limited democracy. Military junta. Ruthless dictatorship. Who could stand against us? Oh, we might have to put down a rebellion of officers loyal to Awak and the things he stands for. But that shouldn't be a big problem. We could tell lies and get loyalty from most of the army. They would only learn later that we had no intention of sharing any power or giving the people any rights. Actually, things ought to go quite well for us. We would end up with absolute power."

"Exactly," Mannheim said. But he had heard the tone in my voice.

"On the other hand," I continued, "I made a kind of promise to Awak when I took this job, and that promise extends to the people he represents. Awak is paying me to fight to preserve a way of life here, Mannheim, and I haven't delivered on my end of that contract."

"To hell with your contract," Mannheim said, his face more grim now. "That's all behind you, Rainey. You're not bound to that anymore. Awak is almost dead. You're dealing now with people like his daughter and Mataafa. You owe them nothing."

"I owe the legitimate government of Samoa," I said. I lowered the register of my voice. "And I intend to deliver, Mannheim. I expect to fight you and beat you. Unless you decide to get on a plane and fly out of here and never come back."

Mannheim had sat back on his chair, and now regarded me with a hard, cold look. "I misjudged you, Rainey. I thought you had some brains, as well as guts."

Rabbit had turned back to us, and wore a psychotic look on his narrow face, a look of pure hatred.

"Well, you live and learn," I told him. "But I want to warn you, Mannheim. If we go to battle, we're going out there to win. And because of what you've done before to us, we won't be taking any prisoners. We'll be going for the jugular. We'll particularly be looking for you, and this animal over here." I jerked my thumb at Rabbit.

Suddenly Rabbit drew the Magnum on his hip and aimed it at me. "Let me kill him now!" he hissed out. "I told you about him! Let me blow his frigging head off!"

My two guards quickly raised their assault rifles toward Rabbit, and suddenly guns were bristling everywhere. I looked back at Mannheim. A tic jumped in his cheek as he fought for emotional control.

"No, Rabbit," he said after a moment that seemed like an hour. "Put the gun away."

Rabbit wasn't going to do it. He had vowed to kill

me at the first chance, and he had missed that chance at Mafili. His eyes were wild.

"I said put the gun away," Mannheim said firmly now.

Rabbit paused, then finally jammed the gun back into its holster. He was breathing shallowly. I think he would have risked his own life at that moment to kill me.

"High-caliber officers you have under you, Mannheim," I said sourly to him. "You're going to need a lot of luck before this is over."

Mannheim was getting his own emotions stabilized. He took a deep breath in and let it out slowly. "Maybe Rabbit's judgment is not of the best at certain moments," he said. "But he and all of my people are good at one thing, Rainey. Killing. I hope you remember that."

"I haven't forgotten," I said.

"It's too bad you don't have more sense, Rainey," he went on. "This could all have been so much easier. Lives could have been saved, lives you pretend to worry about. The fact is, you enjoy directing other men in battle so much, you're willing to risk their deaths rather than take a reasonable way out. But I still have one last offer to make you."

I looked at a watch on my wrist. "Make it faster than the first one, Mannheim. I'm expected back at HQ."

"All right, here it is, and fast. I have a lot of money in back of me, Rainey. I can offer you many times the sum that you're being paid by Awak, no matter what it is."

I don't know why I asked. I guess I just felt

devilish at the moment. "What would be your top offer, Mannheim?" I said.

He thought a momont. "How about a cool million?" he suggested. "Just to leave Samoa and get on with your questionable career. Or go into business, or retire, or whatever you like. You could do just about what you wanted, Rainey. I could deliver the money to a Swiss bank of your choosing, within a week."

I grunted. "It's a tempting offer," I admitted.

"Only a damned fool would refuse it," he said.

"That's the first time I've ever been offered payment for not doing something," I said. "It makes me feel kind of important."

I rose from my chair, with Mannheim and Rabbit watching my face closely. I turned toward my driver and guards, who could hear everything that was being said. They looked worried. The morning was so tranquil that you would find it impossible to believe a bloody battle could ever take place there.

"But I have to turn you down, Mannheim," I said finally.

"Shit," Rabbit spat out at me.

I looked over at him. "You ought to be glad, Rabbit. Now you'll have that last chance at me you've wanted so badly."

"You're making a foolish decision, Rainey," Mannheim said.

"I know," I told him. "But if I survive this, it's one I can live with."

Mannheim rose too. "Then I guess our meeting is over," he said. "The next time we meet, Rainey, it will be you or us."

"That's that way I see it," I said.

He had regained his composure. "When you get back to your headquarters, say hello to Colonel Tupua for me."

I grinned slightly. "How thoughtful," I said.

I went back to the jeep and we all got in. Mannheim and Rabbit and their two hired thugs watched us like hawks, and we watched them. No move was made to stop us, though. We drove off watching our backs, and the canvas tent shrank into a dot on the hill.

"Well," I said to the driver. "That was a waste of time. Just like Jake said it would be."

"It was brave of you to go, General," the driver said.

We were out of sight of the meeting site in seconds, and I felt a little relieved that nobody had tried to stop us. But I had a gut feeling that Mannheim wasn't through with me. In the next five minutes, that feeling was vindicated.

We had come only a mile and a half from the meeting place when it happened. We had to pass another area of rocks, and this time they were waiting for us. A jeepload of rebels had lain in wait there for us, three on either side of the track, behind the rocks. Now suddenly they attacked us with shattering violence, the morning erupting with barking gunfire.

We were caught between a double hail of hot lead, a crossfire from several assault rifles. In the first seconds, my driver was hit in the head, I was shot in the hip, and one of my soldiers in the rear seat was punched in the chest. Bullets clanged off the hot metal of the jeep as I dived to the ground, in sudden pain. I hit the dirt hard, and sand was dug up all around me by rifle fire. My driver slumped onto the steering wheel, dead when the slug hit him. The guard hit in the chest was hanging on, and he and the other man were returning fire bravely. I heard a rebel yell, and then another one.

But we were getting cut to pieces. "*Get off the jeep!*" I yelled to my people. "*Hit the ground!*"

The guy already hit jumped too late. He was caught again, this time in the center back. He flailed his arms and went down beside me. He jumped and jerked there for a moment, and was still. I reached up and grabbed the end of the recoilless rifle and pulled it down to me.

The other guard was on the ground now, on the far side of the jeep, and firing wildly toward his attackers. I fired my Browning and a rebel was hit in the high chest, on my side. He fell onto his face. There was only one rebel on my side now, and he was trying to get his gun unjammed. I picked the recoilless rifle up, primed it, and rested it on the jeep's back bumper. I triggered it in the next second, and it exploded in my hands and hurled a deadly missile toward the three men at the rocks on the far side of the track. They were crouched at their jeep, and suddenly the jeep just lifted into the air in a bright explosion and they went flying in all directions.

I never saw where they all landed, but I knew I had killed all of them. Now the guy on my side had his gun fixed, but he realized that he was suddenly alone. He turned to run, and my other guard fired and hit him in the back of the neck. The rebel yelled once and the yell was cut off as if a TV had been turned off. Then he was lifeless on the ground.

I got up, painfully. So did the soldier with me. He

was unhurt. But when I looked at the other two, it was clear they had bought the farm. The rebels were all dead. I didn't even check them out. I went around the jeep and examined the corpse of the driver. The surviving guard came over to me.

"You are hurt, General?"

I looked at my left hip. There was blood on my trousers. But all I had was a shallow flesh wound there, no bone involved. In a few days, I would be ready for battle.

"It's nothing, soldier," I said. "But Jake was right."

"Yes?"

"He said Mannheim was probably setting me up. Mannheim didn't really believe I'd accept any of his offers." I was talking more to myself than to him. "He got me out here to kill me. It was a death trap, just like Jake thought it might be."

"Yes, sir," the soldier said.

I looked around us. Mannheim was nowhere around. He had thought this ambush would get me. He wouldn't dirty his hands with it. Now the morning was peaceful again. But there were eight dead men lying around the rocky track.

I had to wonder how many lives would be taken in the big battle. And with that hole in my flesh, it occurred to me that one of them might be my own.

Maybe Samoa itself was my death trap, as it had been John Boy's.

I turned to my guard. "Get our soldiers into the jeep," I said. "Our people will be waiting for us back there."

ELEVEN

It took three days for my hip to get in shape so I didn't have to limp when I walked, but it was healing fast, and I kept doped up so I wouldn't feel it. On the fourth day, I thanked my lucky stars that Mannheim hadn't decided to take the offensive in the meantime and gathered my ranking officers to me.

"What's the latest on Mannheim's positions?" I asked in the HQ tent, as we all sat around in a briefing session.

A young Samoan colonel reported to me. "There is no report of obvious troop movement, General," he said. "Except that perhaps the rebels are concentrating their forces centrally."

"Mannheim knows there's going to be one big battle, and that that will decide the war," I said. "He wants to hit us with everything he has available. He knows I'm going to take the offensive. He'll probably hope to suck us in deep, then attack us in force in a pocket where we can't fight our way out. He has the people to do it."

Tupua sat on my left side, Jake on my right. There were two dozen of us at the long table that had been erected in my HQ tent. It was high noon outside, and a slight breeze blew in off the high plains.

A rather elderly colonel spoke up. "I believe we must strike as soon as is possible, General. The advantage will go to the army that makes the first offensive attack."

"There will only be one offensive attack," Tupua told him. "That will engage all the troops on both sides. We will win or lose this war in a matter of a few hours."

"Maybe an hour," Jake said.

"I agree," I told them. "We have to hit them with a goddamn firestorm. I want every available piece of equipment ready, every ambulatory soldier. Tupua, call up our remaining garrison in Apia. All but a few to make sure Leilani Awak and Mataafa are in check there. I want to throw a tornado at Mannheim."

"Does your previous order still stand?" a middle-aged colonel wanted to know. "About not taking prisoners?"

"Does anybody have any objection to that?" I asked.

There was silence around the table.

"Then the order stands," I said.

"Should we leave the capital undefended?" another colonel asked.

I shrugged. "Mannheim doesn't want Apia. He wants us. Even if he could get past us to take Apia, what good would it do him? No, this war will be won or lost right out here in the field. Mannheim is well aware of that."

I nodded at Crazy Jake, and he got up and walked over to a map stand and drew the map down so it was displayed to the table. He picked up a pointer and placed the tip of it on the map.

"Over the past couple of days, we've moved troops out all along this front, as you all know. In both directions from HQ. Our companies all along that line are well equiped now with M85c's, grenade-launchers, recoilless rifles, and rocket mortars. We have two operable rocket cannons, and we've placed them with Comapnies A and M. Here and here." He pointed with the stick.

Tupua spoke up. "We were waiting for word on Mannheim's field-piece capacity," he said.

"So far we've seen no cannon," Jake told the assemblage. "So that's a plus for us. But they do have three or four armored cars to our single one. They can be dangerous, as we found out at Mafili. We think their armored cars are spread out over Mannheim's spreading front line."

"We'll keep our combat car here centrally," I put in. "I expect Mannheim's strength to be central, and we'll need all the firepower we can assemble right at this mile marker."

"We think Mannheim has placed his seasoned troops in these positions marked here, here, and here," Jake went on. He touched the pointer to some topographically rocky areas. He turned to us. "Rainey and I found out that these people can fight. They like to kill, and they're good at it. We have a couple of companies more than the rebels, but they have the experience, and they're all tough men. Our people have to know that. This won't be any goddamn Marquis of Queensbury fight. It will be dirty and ugly, by God. We've got to be ready for that."

Jake stuck an unlighted cigar into his mouth and moved back to his chair and slumped onto it. There was a brief silence among the officers, as they thought over what Jake had told them. None of them were seasoned battle veterans either. It was only Jake and me. That's the way it usually was, in these little wars where mercenaries were hired.

I got up and walked over to the map. "Mannheim has a weak point in his line, as Jake and I see it. Right here." I pointed at a spot on the map to the east of battalion HQ. "If he has any green troops, they're bunched there. Also, there's no armored car within two miles of that spot, so far as we can see."

I was smoking one of the thin Cuban cigars. I took it from my mouth and blew a ring into the still air of the tent. "That's where we're hitting with everything we've got," I said.

There was a low murmuring among them, mostly of approval.

"I'm going to take two companies and Jake will lead two others. We'll go in side by side, and we'll hit them like a goddamn hurricane. Our objective: to split off the rebel outlying companies—two of them—out here, and surround them while the rest of our force occupies Mannheim here centrally, armored car and mortars and everything."

"I like it," a young officer said.

"It ought to work, General," Tupua offered.

"A very sound strategy," a third man told me.

They were probably more convinced than me.

Strategies have a way of blowing up in your face. Both Jake and I had found that out on more than one occasion. But these colonels and majors were relying on me to be smart, trusting me to be as clever as Mannheim, and I had convinced them I was. Now all I had to do was convince myself.

"If we are successful in surrounding these flanking companies," an older colonel asked, "what happens to those men so trapped?"

I looked around at their grim faces. I knew they wanted to hear my resolve, and I gave it to them. "You know the resolution," I said. "Everybody in that circle will be a dead man."

I saw the satisfaction on their faces.

"Don't make any mistake about it," I said. "Mannheim is playing for keeps. If any of our people surrender to him, he'll kill them, either now or later. If we had any doubts about that, I think they were removed when he went back to Mannheim. And when he sent John Boy back to us."

"Amen," Jake grunted.

"This will be a fight to the death," I said. "As an army and as individuals. You either win or you lose big. I didn't dictate those terms. Mannheim did. Don't forget it, and don't forget what kind of man Mannheim is."

"We are not about to, General," Tupua told me solemnly.

"Once we've cut off and destroyed that smaller segment of Mannheim's army," I said, "we'll turn back on him centrally. Our western companies will have moved up and engaged his and hopefully overcome them, so that our second phase of the battle will be to close in on Mannheim's main force from three directions. The only thing he will be able to do is fight or run to the sea. Either way, we'll be all over him. Any questions?"

"When do we go, General?" the young colonel asked me.

I glanced around the room at their tense faces. "Tomorrow morning," I said. "Two hours before dawn."

There was a loud murmuring response in the confines of the tent.

"I know your reaction. I know it well. You think maybe it's too soon, you think you're not ready. You're scared. Who the hell wouldn't be? But the time is right."

"But two hours before dawn!" an older officer challenged me. "Nobody fights in the dark, General. We won't be able to see who we're shooting at."

"Our eyes will be accustomed to the dark by then," I told him. "We'll be up at two. We'll also make good use of the starlight scopes we just got delivered to us. We won't see as well as we would at noon, of course. But with a little luck, the enemy will just be getting out of bed."

"Sleepy and groggy," Crazy Jake grinned. "That kind of enemy makes a great target."

"It is a good plan," Tupua backed me. "I for one am eager to put it into action."

There was a lot of concurrences then, and spirit seemed good.

"Okay," I said. "I'll see you all at two tomorrow morning. Taps will be at eight tonight, pass the word down. With a little luck, we'll have Mannheim beat by sunup."

"I'm counting on it," Tupua smiled at me.

There wasn't much sleep that night, despite the early curfew. After taps I could see men sitting out in front of their tents in the dark, discussing in quiet tones. They were preparing for what was coming, for possible death. Each man had his own way of dealing with it, and I didn't interfere.

An orderly woke me at 1:30 in the black of the night, and I swore when I learned it was raining lightly. I had a cup of black coffee with Crazy Jake, and he was very quiet. Out in the encampment, activity began accelerating. Trucks and jeeps growled around the place in new mud, and equipment was loaded. The heavy field pieces were left with Tupua at HQ when we moved out at 3:30 to the east, Jake and I. We took four light companies and were equipped like a commando force. If Mannheim's outlying companies had field equipment, we could be in trouble, but I didn't think they did.

We donned kevlar helmets and strapped on sidearms and gunbelts and headed out to the east in a light, drizzling rain. At the same time, a couple of young colonels headed out west with three companies of regulars, to try to flank Mannheim on the west while we were attacking the soft spot I had spoken of. Tupua and other colonels would move forward against Mannheim's main force in a frontal attack at mid-morning, whether our end runs worked or not. With some luck they would, and we would come at him from south, west, and east.

At 3:45 the rain let up, and at 3:55 we hauled up in a tight bunch just a few hundred yards from the weak spot in Mannheim's line. No scout or sentry had seen us yet, because of the darkness and the rain. We gathered quietly, drawing trucks up that had recoilless rifles mounted on their cabs, and setting eight rocket mortars in place. It was still pitch black, no moon.

At 4:03 Jake walked up to me and took a cigar from his mouth and dropped it to the ground. "We're ready," he said.

"I see that," I said. "Well. Take care of yourself, Jake."

"I always do," he grinned.

I rubbed at my aching hip, and turned to a sergeant with a walkie-talkie transceiver. "Commence mortar fire," I said.

He nodded, and transmitted the message to my mortar people. There was still a moment of silence after that, with our equipment hulking there black in the night and the silhouettes of tents and equipment looming on the near horizon, the encampment of the enemy. Then the night darkness was split wide open by the bright-yellow explosions of rocket mortars, and the sky was rent with the flaming trail of the rockets as they roared off to their targets. There were further explosions at the enemy's camp then as our rockets landed, and then we were into the middle of it.

More rockets blasted off, and commands were shouted, and trucks began moving forward. Antitank recoilless rifles fired their big rounds off into the night, and found targets on the other end.

We softened them up like that only briefly, then the command was given to attack.

Bugles blared, and men shouted.

"*Attack!*" I yelled over the din of noise. "*Go in with everything! Give them hell!*"

Then trucks and jeeps roared on in, and as they got close to the camp, they disgorged wild troops, yelling for blood. Jake and I went in with the first of them, and in moments we were there. The encampment was really an extension of the ones for the remote companies to the east, so we were waking up three companies even though only attacking the one in front of us. Men came stumbling out of tents and a couple of adobe buildings, trying to see in the dark but not able to. My people went in screaming and firing, and the night was filled with the clatter of automatic fire. It was like shooting ducks in a barrel. Most of the enemy didn't even have a weapon to defend themselves with. They went down everywhere, and in big numbers. The mortars had ceased, and now there was only the sound of small fire. A rebel came out of a tent with his pants at his ankles and fired an automatic pistol at my head. It missed and I put him down with a short burst from my M-16. My people were running wild around me, shooting and killing. Tents were set afire to scare out anybody hiding. One rebel came running out afire. Others went running away from us, just to get away from our guns. We cut most of them down. Some got away into the night, but not many. One of our captains had raised a crimson banner in the attack and kept yelling, "*No prisoners!*"

That first part of our attack lasted only minutes, and it was finished. There was dead rebels everywhere, underfoot. But then we turned toward the other two companies, who were now up and out only hundreds of yards away. Our mortars were lobbing rockets into their camp now, and we were getting some incoming in return from them. At a command from me, we turned and went in and around them from all sides, making a pincer movement against them a lot like the kind used by the Zulus against the British at Rourke's Drift.

Now there was heavier fighting. My people started going down around me. I caught a glimpse of Jake, running like hell toward the defending rebels, firing as he ran. Men followed him doing the same thing, and they were hitting a lot of the enemy. Our antitank guns were punching shells into the enemy camp too, and there were a lot of fires burning, smoke curling into the night sky.

In a short time, the rebels began falling back under our withering fire, and it was then that our other people closed in and prevented them from running. The rebels tried all right, but they just ran into crossfire. It was deadly. They began panicking, and running in all directions. We cut them down. A few held up white flags and we cut them down too.

In about an hour, it was over.

I had been grazed on my right leg, but it was just a scratch. I had forgotten my hip completely during the fighting, but now it began aching again. I went and leaned against an enemy truck that was disabled and lit up a cigar. My face was dirt-smeared, and blood caked on my pants leg. The assault rifle hung from my left hand, empty of ammo.

I looked around. The ground was absolutely littered with corpses. Maybe a few rebels had gotten out of our trap, but not many. You couldn't walk on the ground in places, you had to step on corpses. There were arms and legs separated from bodies, and heads mashed and destroyed completely. Faces were blown off. There were literally pools of blood you had to walk through, that dyed your boots black. The air stank of gunpowder and blood.

I looked up and saw Jake limping over to me. He came up and jerked a cigar out of my tunic pocket.

"Now that's what I call a firefight," he grinned crookedly.

He had blood running down the side of his face from his hair, and did not even seem to notice it. He stuck the cigar into his mouth and did not bother to light it.

"Are you all right?" I said.

"Hell, yes. Why, don't I look it?"

"You look okay," I said. "But you're bleeding from the head."

He touched the blood on the side of his face. "Shit, I've done worse than that shaving in the morning."

I rubbed at my hip and made a face. "Sometimes I think we're getting too old for this, Jake."

He nodded. "It's a kid's game, all right," he said. "but the kids don't know how to play it."

I gave the order to start cleaning up, getting help to our wounded. There were no enemy wounded. My people had seen to that. We spent the next hour loading wounded onto trucks and getting them first aid. I tried to get through to Tupua, but couldn't get a response. Finally, just as dawn was streaking the eastern sky with color, a sergeant with a field radio came running up to me.

"There is a coded message from battalion HQ, General. I took it all down."

Jake came up just as I took the piece of paper and read what the sergeant had written on it.

Attack on left flank failed, it read. *Mannheim*

relieved his people in force. Our assault force largely destroyed. Mannheim now coming after us, and has momentum. Day could be lost if you can't hit Mannheim from the east immediately. Our people fighting hard but issue in doubt. Tupua.

I handed the note to Jake, and he read it, scowling. "For Christ's sake," he growled. "That's the trouble with sending boys to do men's work."

"Let's get loaded up and get out of here," I said. "Every minute could count now."

Within ten minutes we were rolling out, leaving death and destruction in our wake. This time our vehicles roared over the rocky terrain fast, bumping and pounding over the rough ground. The rebel company to the west of us had retreated back into the center of Mannheim's line, so we met no opposition for a couple of miles, and then it was light. A mortar squad had been left to slow us up, but we took them out with one well-placed antitank shot. Rebels went flying in all directions, and then we rolled on.

In another three miles we ran into the fighting. We could see the two sides squared off against each other, as we came up against their flanks. Rebels were charging our troops on foot, like madmen. It looked like our people were giving ground too. From my jeep I used the binoculars and could look down the line of battle for a couple of miles. There were yellow explosions in the now-bright sun, and a continuing clatter of small-arms fire. Banners waved in the breeze and bugles blew and there was the yelling of men from both sides.

I stood up in the jeep as my equipment rolled up in a line even with my lead vehicle. I held up my arm.

"There they are! Giving our people hell! What do you say we give some back to them?"

A roar of approval rose from my troops and officers. They had just tasted the blood of the enemy, and they were hyped up to kill.

Jake drew up in a jeep just a few yards away, and waved a red cloth on the end of his rifle. *"Remember Mafili!"* he yelled out.

They roared it back to him. *"Remember Mafili!"*

"No prisoners!" he helled again.

"No prisoners!" came the loud response.

A moment later we swarmed down on the enemy.

They didn't even see us at first, either side. Then we were there, and those rebels that were so excitedly killing government troops turned and saw they were being attacked from the flank. Our people saw it too, and were given incentive to fight back. In moments we joined the battle in force, and the rebels collapsed before the fury of our attack.

"Remember Mafili!"

The chorus kept ringing out as we hit them. The rebels didn't know who to shoot at first, us or the main force they were attacking. We just rolled over them, on foot and in vehicles. They fell fast and hard under our increased fire. Some started running, toward the bigger companies at center, where Mannheim was trying to break Tupua's forces with a wild attack.

I stayed in the jeep, and we fired furiously as we drove. One of my people was shot off the vehicle and then was run over by the truck that was following behind us. I was trying to get into the center of things, to face down Mannheim's hardened center.

In moments we were there. There were enemy

guns all around us, and trucks and jeeps. Rebels swarmed on foot. Out about three hundred yards to the west I caught a glimpse of Mannheim himself on a hillside, shouting orders into a transceiver, standing under a rebel banner. He had already seen our counterattack and was trying to do something to stop it. Two armored cars advanced slowly on us, firing off small field rounds and filling the air with .50-caliber machinegun fire.

A lot of my people were going down. I shouted at a truck crew near me. "*Those goddamn armored cars! Take them out of it! Now!*"

My crew fired at the nearest car and missed. I fired off a clattering series of rounds toward the other one, and bullets whined off its hard metal and did no damage. Our antitank guns and the armored cars began a deadly duel. I saw my nearest truck explode and disintegrate, metal and flesh going everywhere. Our other near one finally hit an armored car in a vulnerable place and it exploded into flame.

"*Drive on!*" I ordered my driver. "*Head toward Mannheim!*"

My driver looked at me like I was crazy, but he followed orders. Even if I lost the goddamn war, I wanted a chance to kill the sonofabitch that had started the whole thing. That would give me real satisfaction, to kill Mannheim. We headed on into a hail of lead, and I heard it whining off the metal of the jeep. My other rifleman in the rear seat was hit and slumped dead back there. My driver was hit in the arm, but kept going.

Our attack was making a big difference now, and I saw government squads moving forward against the rebels. We were turning a defeat into victory, it appeared.

"There! Up there!" I yelled at my driver, pointing toward where Mannheim stood in his jeep.

My driver was almost disabled, but he followed orders. Halfway up the rise, with shells exploding around us and bullets flying, Mannheim saw us coming. There was a machinegun on his vehicle, and he now directed fire directly at us. The hot lead flew, and suddenly my driver was hit again, in the face. The jeep jerked sidewise and turned over on its side.

I threw myself clear at the last moment, wrenching my shoulder and hurting the hip again. I lay on the ground on my face for a moment, and the slugs stopped coming. When I looked up, I saw our troops heading up the hillside, hitting the rebels hard now. Rebel troops were retreating and falling all along the short battle line. When I squinted to see Mannheim, his vehicle was turning and heading away, toward a couple of stone buildings at the edge of a line of thin woods.

"Sonofabitch," I muttered to myself.

Just as I picked myself up, our armored car drove up, guns blazing, and stopped near me. Tupua's torso jutted from the top of it.

"General!" he yelled out.

"I'm all right," I said to him. I grabbed my automatic rifle and hopped aboard the car with considerable effort. "That's Mannheim heading off there. Let's go for him."

Tupua shouted an order to our driver, and we were off again. Rebels were retreating in full force now, but not many were getting away. Our people were slaughtering them with every moment that passed. Our training had paid off after all.

Mannheim's jeep had disappeared behind the nearest building at the tree line. We moved up on it more cautiously now. I ordered the armored car stopped. There were four soldiers aboard besides the driver, and I got off with them. "You stay here to direct fire as necessary, Tupua," I said to him.

Tupua scowled at me. "You are wounded, Rainey. I will lead the assault on the building." He got off the car and strode toward me openly, ignoring some scattered gunfire from that direction.

"Goddamn it, Tupua," I said. "I know the way these bastards fight. I'm giving you a direct order. Stay here and—"

In that instant, a sniper bullet hit Tupua in the high chest.

Tupua slammed against the front of the armored car and hung there, his face going white. I swore under my breath, and grabbed him and dragged him to the rear of the vehicle. I set him down on the ground there and leaned him against it. I examined the wound, and was relieved to see that it was high, and had missed his aorta.

He was muttering some choice Samoan obscenities under his breath. I had to hand it to him, he had guts.

"You're one lucky colonel, my friend," I told him. "But that sniper ended our argument. Stay put here and I'll get you medical help immediately. You ought to be safe until help arrives."

"Forget the medics," Tupua frowned, gasping in pain. "Just get the job finished, Rainey."

"Don't worry, we will," I told him.

One of my people returned to find a medic, and the other three and I crept up on the rear building. Some scattered fire came from that direction. We hit the dirt, and the firing stopped.

"All right," I said to the others. "Let's go in."

We got to our feet and ran toward the building. No fire greeted us. When we arrived we took cover at the building wall, and then I risked a look inside through a window.

I could see right through a rear doorway to the back, and there were rebels back there preparing to leave in vehicles.

"*Come on!*" I yelled. "*They're getting away!*"

We ran for the rear of the building, and as soon as we got there, one of my people went down, hit in the belly by a rebel aboard a nearby jeep. A second jeep was driving away, and I saw Mannheim aboard. I raised my rifle to fire after it, but it crested a rise of ground and disappeared. The driver of the second jeep started the engine as two uniformed rebels fired at us. One of the two was Rabbit Burroughs.

Rabbit fired off a volley from an assault rifle and caught my second soldier in the middle chest. He was thrown off his feet violently and was dead when he hit the ground beside me. The rebel beside Rabbit was knocked off the jeep by my last man, and then I raked the car with fire and hit him and Rabbit. The other rebel went flying into the weeds, but Rabbit was jut grazed on the arm. He returned my fire, his pink-blue eyes wild with fury when he saw me. He fired at me and my last man and hit the guy in both legs. He went down near me. I rolled once and fired again, shattering the windshield on Rabbit's jeep and killing his driver just as the guy was about to drive off. The radiator was steaming now too, and it was clear that Rabbit was not going to drive away from there. I squeezed the trigger a last time and the firing pin clicked on an empty chamber. I was out of ammo. I saw Rabbit inspecting his weapon, and knew he had done the same thing. He was not wearing a sidearm, and I had lost mine.

I rose from the ground and faced Rabbit. He looked up from the weapon and stared at me for a moment, then threw the gun to the ground. He jumped off the jeep and glared at me.

"Well, Rabbit. We get a second chance at this," I said.

"That suits me right down to the ground, Rainey," he hissed out at me. He had lost his military hat, and his white hair made a wild halo above his head—an irony that did not escape me.

He reached into the jeep and pulled out a long tire iron, and turned back to me with a slight grin. I looked around and saw a short length of steel chain somebody had left behind. I grabbed it at each end, so that there was about two feet between as I held it.

"That won't help you this time, Rainey. You don't have a grenade-launcher to save your ass now. I'm going to mash you, goddamn it. I'm going to break every goddamn bone in your body, and then start on your insides. I'm going to beat your frigging brains out."

"Don't just talk about it," I invited him. "Do it."

He had moved up on me. Now he swung the iron bar with violent force at my head. I ducked and caught it with the chain, and deflected the blow. He sumbled past me and I released one end of the chain, whipping out with it. It caught him over the shoulder. He yelled and grabbed the chain. With a vicious tug, he pulled me off balance and I went plummeting to the ground at his feet. As I rolled over, I saw the thick bar descend toward my face. I rolled away from it and it thudded heavily onto the ground beside my head. That blow would have crushed my skull like a Samoan papaya, I figured. I grabbed the bar and pulled savagely on it and Rabbit came hurtling to the ground too. He fell just beside me as I twisted the bar loose from his grasp and swung one end at his face just as he turned to grab me.

The iron bar smashed into Rabbit's left eye, popped the eyeball, and drove on into his brain pan, burying itself in his skull for a length of six inches.

The other eye saucered grotesquely, and a shiver of shock ran all through Rabbit's body. I pulled the iron back out of his head and a crimson fountain spurted out behind it. Rabbit fell onto his back, his legs and arms jumping and jerking there for a long moment, his good eye seeming to stare upward at me angrily. Then he was still there on the dirt, his face a bloody mess. His wild hair had mud in it, and the contact lens had fallen out of his good eye. The iris seemed particularly bright pink as he stared skyward.

Rabbit Burroughs had committed his last atrocity in the name of other people's causes.

Now there was only Mannheim himself.

TWELVE

We won the war by the end of that long day on the battleground.

It took a couple more days to mop up the rebels in adjoining villages, but it had been over for all practical purposes by the time Rabbit and I had our deadly duel to the death at that outpost building that bloody day.

By the end of that week, there was no resistance left. Mannheim had run off somewhere and finally abandoned the islands to those who deserved to own it. Crazy Jake had sustained a side wound in addition to the wound to the head that day, but I couldn't get him to admit himself to our military hospital in Apia. He went on a drinking binge for several days after the big battle, and I didn't interfere. He had earned the right.

Dr. Awak surprised me. With news of our winning the war, he found new vitality from somewhere, got out of his sick bed, and returned to his offices in the Government House building. Within forty-eight hours he arranged for the deportation of Leilani and the trial of Mataafa in a civilian court of law. He took charge in a way that I had thought was now beyond his capability, and that pleased me. Also, I visited Tanu in the hospital, and he was recovering so well that he was expected to be discharged within a few days. He insisted on a complete run-down on the action he had missed, and I obliged. He too had earned the right. He wanted to go with me when I left Samoa, fight beside me in any future wars I might involve myself in.

"I'm sorry, Tanu. But I'm a loner. Your place is here, with your people. A lot of rebuilding has to be done. You might end up village chief at Mafili."

"I wish to see the big world out there, Rainey," he insisted. "To have great adventures with you, and take care of you."

I rarely felt any real comradship with another soldier in my business, but I felt very strongly for Tanu. That was why I was just as insistent as he was. "I don't need anybody to take care of me, old friend," I said. "But your people do need you. Very much. Take my word for it, Tanu. This business isn't for you. Your destiny is right here in Samoa. I expect big things of you. I want you to expect big things of yourself."

He finally understood. When I left him that sunny afternoon, it was the last time I ever saw him, and I guess that was just as well. Later in that same day, I met with Dr. Awak in his spacious office.

"Well, Rainey," he said to me when we were seated there, he behind his impressive desk. "You did it. You saved Samoa from Mannheim."

"Me and a lot of other people," I said. "Mostly Samoans."

"I wish you would reconsider staying on," he said. "I could use a man like you, Rainey. This whole government has to be reorganized. The *matai* are very taken with you. I talked with Colonel Tupua today at the hospital and he says you would be a perfect man for a new Defense Minister post. He himself has accepted the post of Deputy Prime Minister vacated by my daughter."

"He deserves the honor," I said.

"Well, Rainey? What about it? We could even find a place for your friend Jake Murphy."

I grinned. The offers kept coming in, even now. "You don't know Jake. Giving him a desk job would be like putting him in jail. No, neither of us is equipped for political leadership. I'll be leaving for Pago Pago tomorrow morning."

"Pago Pago?" Awak frowned. His narrow face had some color in it again, and his eyes held some of the old fire.

I nodded. "I just got word from an imformant. Mannheim has shown up there, Minister. The war isn't quite over yet, it seems. I figured Mannheim had run to Europe, but it seems he hasn't learned his lesson yet. I'm going there to find him, Minister. There will be no extra charge to you."

"That isn't necessary, Rainey. You don't owe us any more involvement."

"I don't feel that way," I said.

"I see."

"I feel I have something to settle between us, anyway," I said. "He let his people do some pretty rotten things. He has to be brought to justice. Somebody has to care."

Awak sighed. "I suppose I can't dissuade you."

"No, Minister," I said. "You can't."

"Would you like to see Leilani before you leave?" he wondered. "She expressed an interest in meeting with you again."

I hesitated. "I guess not," I said.

"I understand." He watched me puff on the cigar. "Will you come back through here after dealing with Mannheim? If you live through your last confrontation with him?"

I grinned at the last. "I doubt it, Minister. Jake says he can get us work in Chad, fighting Qadaafi's army there. That sounds like the kind of thing I might like. I'm to meet Jake in L.A. in less than a week, if I'm interested. If I don't get there, he'll go alone."

Awak smiled at me. "You really are one of a kind, Jim Rainey. It has been a pleasure knowing you."

"The pleasure is mutual, Minister," I told him.

It was a couple of hours later that I found Crazy Jake at a local bar. He had just arrived a half-hour before, and he was sober. I sat down and ordered a drink with him and we drank slowly without talking. He had already removed the Samoan uniform and was wearing a khaki shirt and trousers again. There was a bandage on the side of his head, but otherwise he looked as good as ever.

Finally I looked over at him. "How long will you stay in L.A.?"

He grunted. He looked tough and ugly across the table. He was one of the best damned soldiers I had ever fought with or against. "A few days. Longer if you want me to.'

"No," I said. "If I'm not there by the tenth, take off. They're paying good wages in Chad."

He swigged the rest of the brandy. "You're usually not such a goddamn fool, Rainey."

I looked over at him.

"You don't have to go after Mannheim. You did the job you were paid for. You're breaking a basic rule, taking on more than you were paid to do. It ain't professional."

I smiled. "This doesn't have to do with pay, Jake," I said. "It has to do with John Boy."

"Shit, that's between mercs, what you're talking about. Mannheim's no professional soldier."

"He fits the description close enough. I can't let him get off like this, Jake. For Samoa or for us."

Jake shrugged. "It's your business," he said.

I nodded, and rose. "I'll see you in L.A.," I said.

He wouldn't look up at me. "You're screwing with your luck, Rainey. He'll kill you if he gets just half a chance."

"Until L.A., Jake," I said.

"Right," he said, still not meeting my eye.

I left him sitting there looking mean. I guessed that even Crazy Jake was finally feeling something for another merc. Maybe that war in Samoa had been good for both of us, I thought.

The next morning early I flew off to Pago Pago. I knew that Jake was leaving for the States later that same day. I arrived in Pago Pago in mid-morning and took a leisurely hour finding a room at a local hotel. I was in no hurry. If Mannheim was there, I'd find him soon enough.

I was right. In early afternoon, I found a bartender who had seen Mannheim just the night before. He had been in the place drinking with another man.

"Who is this other man?" I said.

"Hell, some guy by the name of Slade," the thick-set barman told me. "He's just some bum that showed up a couple of weeks ago. Got in two brawls in the first three days. Drinks a lot at that place across the street too."

He pointed to the bar where John Boy and I had sat drinking when we first laid eyes on Mannheim. That seemed like about a thousand years ago.

"Does he come in here every day?" I said.

"No," he said. "But there he is now."

I looked to where he was pointing, and saw the husky guy walk through the swinging doors. He looked like an American, and was wearing blue jeans and a leather vest over a plaid shirt, with boots of some kind under the jeans. He swaggered over the to bar. I beat the bartender to him.

"Your name Slade?" I said.

"That's right," he said, looking me over arrogantly. "Who wants to know?"

"I'm looking for Fredrik Mannheim," I said. "Can you tell me where to find him?"

He paused. "Yeah," he said.

"Well?"

"Well what?" he said.

I was getting irritated. "Well, where the hell can I find him?"

He let a hard grin move his heavy features. "I said I can tell you. Not that I will."

I held my temper. I reached into a pocket, and put a wad of bills on the bar. "Will that make any difference?"

He studied the wad for a moment, then shrugged. He took the money. "He's holed up in a guest house only two blocks from here. It's got a sign on the front. The Deauville, I think they call it." He turned away from me. "Now butt out, jerk."

I sighed. "Sure," I said. "There's just one other thing."

He turned back sourly. "Yeah?"

I jammed stiff knuckles into his Adam's apple, without warning.

His eyes saucered, and he stumbled away from the bar, choking and gasping for breath, holding his throat. When he came past me, I threw an elbow into his side and a rib cracked audibly. He yelled through the choking and hit the floor on his face.

I reached down and grabbed the money from him, and turned to a wide-eyed bartender. "Here," I said. "You earned this. He didn't."

The guy nodded numbly. I turned and left the place, with the drifter still scrabbling on the floor, trying to get up but unable to.

In just five minutes I stood outside the Deauville. It was a rundown private residence of two stories, with weathered clapboard siding and a metal roof that was starting to rust through. There were louvered hurricane shutters at the windows, and the house stood off the ground on three-foot brick pilings.

The front door was closed behind a ragged screen, and it looked as if the owner was not at home. I climbed several steps and tried to look in. I saw nothing. I took out the Browning Mark I that I had acquired in my Samoan war, and fitted a three-inch silencer to it that Awak had procured for me. I descended the steps and moved around to the rear of the place on a concrete walk.

Behind the house was an outside stairway to an upstairs room or suite. I thought I heard sounds from up up there. A couple of louvered windows were open. I loaded the Browning by drawing the slide ejector back and releasing it with a metallic clicking. I was ready.

It took only moments to quietly climb the stairs. When I arrived on a platform outside the door to the place, I distinctly heard men's voices inside. One of the voices belonged to Fredrik Mannheim. I sneaked a look through the louvers in the door, and saw them in there. Mannheim was sitting propped on a bed with pillows behind him. He was wearing a gunbelt and was armed. Not far from him sat a bearded guy at a table, swigging liquor from a bottle. He looked tough. I couldn't see a gun, but his kind usually carried one.

I listened.

". . . and that means we'd have the same potential here," Mannheim was saying. "We'd start here instead of Apia. Once we got control here, we could spread out into the whole South Pacific. I see a goddamn empire out here some day. With my people running it."

"It might work," the other man said. Despite the booze, he was sober. "As I told you before, I could get some help from a couple of families. I ain't done all that wasting for them for nothing. I can get the ear of Angelo Bernini, for example. It would be a whole new world for the rackets out here, and I think he'd go for it. All we'd need is his money backing and some choice people to help us recruit."

"I'd have to retain complete autonomy," Mannheim said. "This would be a business deal, not a takeover."

"Hey," the other guy said. "I'd make all that clear."

So that was it. Mannheim had latched onto a Mafia hit man to hook him up with more financial backing. As a way to continue his plan to tyrannize the South Pacific. Despite his loss in Samoa.

I realized, standing there, that if I didn't do something to stop him in his tracks once and for all, Mannheim still might realize that dream. With the kind of help he was seeking.

That made my resolve steady. I took a deep breath in, stepped back from the door for a moment, and told myself this was it. There was nothing for it but to do it.

With a violent kick, I smashed at the door and it went flying inward. I came in behind it quick, as both Mannheim and the assassin came to their feet, going for guns on their hips.

I aimed at Mannhem first because he had his Luger out and aimed at my chest. The Browning popped loudly and Mannheim was hit in the high chest. He was dumped back onto the bed hard, and his hand hit the headboard and the Luger went flying.

Still in a low crouch, I saw the hit man aim and fire a heavy automatic at me. A slug tore at my collar as the gun barked out in the room, and then I squeezed off two more rounds. The first one caught the killer in the stomach, and the second one hit him just over the heart. He went down hard, taking the table and two chairs with him.

I rose slowly from the crouch. Both men were down. The hit man was dead, sprawled not far away with a look of abject surprise on his killer's face, his eyes wide open. A trickle of blood wormed from his mouth.

Mannheim had slid to the floor and was sitting half-propped against he bed, holding his hand over the wound in his high chest. I had not hit him in a vital place, and he was still very much alive, but out of it. He watched me as I moved past him, the smoking Browning hanging loosely at my side.

"I'll be damned," he grated out. "You followed me."

I did not respond. I walked to the other room and looked into it, and into a bathroom. There were no more of them. I came back and stood over Mannheim, the Browning still in my hand.

"I don't know why you bothered, Rainey," he said through his teeth.

"Yeah?" I said.

"That's right. What good did this do you? You didn't shoot straight enough, Rainey. Now you have a wounded prisoner on your hands, and you play by the rules. You're not going to kill me in cold blood now, it's not in you. That is why—" He coughed. "That is why men like me will always win over those like you, in the long run. You don't have the same resolve we do, Rainey. You can't stop me. You'll turn me over to the authorities here, or just leave me, and I'll go to hospital and recover and then I'll continue in just the way I always have, until my goals are accomplished. Do you see the irony of it all?"

I raised the Browning and shot Mannheim in the head.

His head whiplashed against the bed, and then he was staring up at me in utter disbelief as he slid over onto his side.

I stood over him for a long moment. "Yes, I play by the rules, you sonofabitch. But you forgot an important rule between us. No prisoners."

I hid the Browning again under my bush tunic, and left the place. There was nobody around outside. Apparently no one had heard the Mafia man's gun go off. That was good for me. I wanted to get out of Pago Pago without explanations. I'd fly to L.A. and meet Crazy Jake there, and we'd have some drinks together and remember Samoa. Maybe we'd send off a card to an uncle John Boy had mentioned, telling what had happened to him.

Then we'd go off to some other war together.

You might not think that was something great to look forward to.

But it was what we had.